Books by Gina Apostol

Bibliolepsy

The Revolution According to Raymundo Mata

Gun Dealers' Daughter

Insurrecto

BIBLIOLEPSY

Gina Apostol

First published by University of Philippines Press.

This edition first published in 2022 by
Soho Press, Inc.
227 W 17th Street
New York, NY 10011

Library of Congress Cataloging-in-Publication Data
Apostol, Gina, author.
Bibliolepsy / Gina Apostol.

ISBN 978-1-64129-251-1
eISBN 978-1-64129-252-8

LCC PR9550.9.A66 B63 2022 | DDC 823'.914—dc23
LC record available at https://lccn.loc.gov/2021018960

Interior design by Janine Agro, Soho Press, Inc.

Printed in the United States of America

10 9 8 7 6 5 4 3 2 1

For Arne

BIBLIOLEPSY

Author's Note on the US Edition

On the anniversary of what Filipinos now call the EDSA Revolt, the week in February 1986 when a prolonged street rebellion in Manila saw the fall of the Marcos family, the "conjugal dictatorship" that had ruled the country for some two decades, I sometimes look up this passage to see if it still matters. To be honest, I wish it did not.

> "It was at about this time . . . that the country became afflicted with what one might call *semiosis*, a sepsis of the semiotic tract, an infection of the sign-making glands. We assign to this event meanings that all lead to questions of life and death, philosophical heartburn and patriotic dread. We revise and revisit our feelings toward it the way Romans of old found omens in the intestines of birds. That, too, was a form of semiosis. The street itself, EDSA, takes on, at odd moments in the present day when I travel through it, a weirdly disorienting sense of a symbol gone awry. Why should it? It's still just a street, going to seed in an unremarkable third world way.
>
> "Other people (e.g., psychoanalysts, romance

novelists, air traffic controllers) have pointed out before in different contexts that the ability to see meanings is not necessarily a sign of wisdom, or health. It may indicate intellectual training or acumen, yes, but it may also be a symptom of delusion, fierce heartache, severe ennui, and other renditions of mental weakness. We must take into account that our own revisions of the rebellion we call, eponymously and thoughtlessly, *EDSA* may be all of the above, and more."

I CHANGED NOTHING much in this edition of *Bibliolepsy*, though I wish I could have changed the above paragraphs, in the sense that—I wish that the country truly had moved on, become the state of democracy and justice that our banners then wished it to be.

Maybe because *Bibliolepsy* is my first novel, its syntax is etched in me. I carried it so long in my head in the years I began writing it—I was nineteen in August, 1983, when I first conceived of writing about this neurological neologism, this condition, bibliolepsy. Yes, the made-up word mixes up the Latin and the Greek in the way of the amateur. A novel only about desire. And that was odd because the streets of the country (or at least its old capital, Manila) were finally turning outward, toward revolt, because of an assassination in broad daylight, on an airport tarmac.

Etched in my mind, too, is the moment my good friend, a classmate in creative writing workshops, Cochise Bernabe (yes, this privileged son of the vice-mayor of Pasay, friend of movie stars and a capella crooner of Broadway songs, who carried around *The Preppie Handbook* that he had bought on his last visit to New York, whose real name was Ernesto, nicknamed himself after the great Apache chief)—Cochise asked me if I wanted to join him and his choral group at the airport to serenade Ninoy Aquino.

It was Open House at my dorm, Kamia. The all-women's dorm lounge was swarming with his pink and lime Lacoste-shirt-wearing fellow chorus members, "brods" of his fraternity, which was also the frat of former senator Aquino, exiled by their other fellow frat member, the dictator Ferdinand Marcos.

I barely registered that this senator was coming home.

I looked at Cochise with horror. Are you kidding me, I said.

I had only scorn for Ninoy Aquino.

I was a teenage Maoist, as far as one could be Maoist when mainly one wished to write novels. (It's pretty clear how *Bibliolepsy*'s protagonist is not me.) My sympathies were with farmers and laborers and student activists who had long been agitating against the US-Marcos dictatorship, as our banners called the Philippines's fascist government propped up by American military money in my Cold War childhood. I believed in activists on the ground, not politicians on a plane. Ninoy Aquino was no people's hero. He was an upper-class landowner-politician who married into one of the richest families in the country, and in my view, his return home was a sop, a bourgeois political spectacle removed from my concerns.

A frat rumble among the upper classes.

Thus, my ideological rigidity made me miss history.

The morning after Ninoy Aquino's assassination—a shameless murder that awakened people to join activists and protest their government, until it fell three years later—I remember seeing Cochise at the covered walk leading to the Faculty Center, where the English department held writing workshops.

How'd the serenade go, I asked him.

Even now I see, in my mind's eye, Cochise's ashen face—his disoriented look, his wide eyes.

In my memory, he had not even changed from his serenading clothes.

Clearly, I had not heard the news.

You see, despite my years marching in street demonstrations at the state university in Diliman, at the same time all I wanted to do, to be honest, was read books and write novels.

I'd hole up for days in my dorm room, not bothering even to go to class, just reading.

It's been thirty-seven years, and I still remember my exchange with Cochise. But rereading that novel I had begun working on then, I believe I was correct in holding on to my sense of those times—this political belief I had, and still have, about the primacy of this plot: the plot of desire. That this grappling with desire lies at the heart of our political imaginations, and to engage in the fullness of its contradictions and vagaries and ineptitudes is also a way toward clarity, or honesty.

Bibliolepsy is meant to be a novel about the cyclical endlessness of desiring. In the case of this novel—the desiring of books, of words. From the start, I conceived of it as a book that would have a sense of never being finished. Both a historical and a personal truth, maybe, resides in such a story.

It's odd to think of the intervening years. Seven years after that morning in August, Cochise was dead, age only twenty-six—in one of those violent Metro Manila incidents of mistaken identity and criminal passion, legally unsolved, that still horrifies. In 1987, Leandro Alejandro, whom we all called Lean (two syllables), the most charismatic, most compelling student leader of my generation, was gunned down, again in broad daylight when, having been a kid sprung from the nationalist left, he decided to run for office in the new regime. Again, his actual killer has not been brought to justice. The year of Leandro Alejandro's death, an unknown, gun-toting lawyer became the officer-in-charge, or transitional mayor, of Davao City in the south, appointed by the new president, the widow Cory Aquino. His mother was a Cory supporter and instead of taking office as mayor, legend now goes the mother asked the president to choose her son. And it's that other man of the EDSA Revolt eighties, that Davao mayor, Rodrigo Duterte, who became president—not Lean, whose political ideas were grounded in historical protest, and not Cochise, who like his idol Ninoy Aquino was from birth brought up to run for president. Instead, decades after, a remnant of EDSA, Duterte, comes to power, perversely honoring the fascist legacy of the first dictator, Marcos, and presiding over, at this count, more than thirty thousand extra-judicial deaths—the killers not brought to justice, just as the Marcoses, in 1986, were not.

There's a sense in this history of a revolt that is not finished.

Though the act of desiring remains.

During the height of those street protests, I sent the opening sheaves of *Bibliolepsy*—the first fifty or so pages of this current book—to a writer I admired, on a lark really. I expected no reply. John Barth wrote *Chimera*, a circular book I loved. At New Manila or Buendia Avenue, I'd hop off from the marches and take detours to the British Council or Thomas Jefferson Cultural Center, imperialist grounds, sure, but places of soft power had books. I'd check out Robert Coover's *The Public Burning* or John Barth's *The Sot-Weed Factor*, or read Auberon Waugh's wicked *Literary Review*. I loved those novels making savage fun of Nixon, or reimagining colonial America, their political wit and literary deftness that, for me, are made powerful by their playful, in my view, postcolonial lens on America. I learned from *Harper's* that this writer Barth actually taught—at a place called Johns Hopkins. And that is how I arrived in the United States, in Baltimore, where I thought I would finish *Bibliolepsy*. I didn't. I got married, I had a child, and I returned home from the States with my young family in the early nineties. Like so many of us women whose years of early creation involve having a child, I finished the novel with maternal angst to spare; but my vow was to finish it with its original vision intact.

When I was ready to send the novel's final version to my first publisher, the University of the Philippines Press, I lost the document on my Apple Macintosh Classic (I still have this infernal machine, in an unreachable attic)—which had no Recovery mode. No computer technician could resurrect that final draft—which included passages I had added because I was researching a new novel, about the 1896 Philippine revolution, and I was so taken with the textual, biblioleptic nature of that war. I published *Bibliolepsy* without those lost paragraphs on Andres Bonifacio, the great bibilioleptic reader of Rizal, and so on. Those lost sections have long made me sad, and I've tinkered with them in my head through the years. I thought—if I have the chance, I'll cobble those paragraphs back in. The additions would barely be noticed given the novel's scheme. Like many writers, I'm an incorrigible reviser, obsessive-compulsively so, but with this novel, apart from my approximations of that lost draft, I hoped to preserve even its sentences' syntax. I made an effort to keep it untouched.

Gina Apostol

September 13, 2020

PART ONE

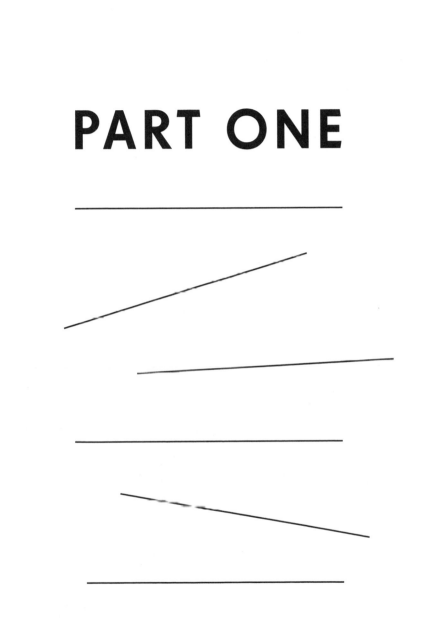

1. Bibliolepsy

Bibliolepsy: a mawkishness derived from habitual aloneness and congenital desire. Manifestations: a quickening between the thighs and in the points of the breast, a broad aching V, when addressed by writers, books, bibliographies, dictionaries, xerox machines, a sympathy for typists of manuscripts. Etymologically related to Humbert Humbert's gross tenderness, though rarely possessing its callous tragedy; occasionally accompanied by a liking for rock and roll. The endless logo-itch, desperately seeking, but it can't get no satisfaction. Biblioleptic attacks usually followed by bouts of complete distaste for words.

2. What I hate about the bibliolept

Name-dropping. The squandering of proper nouns like gaudy wealth. Sure sign of a) amateurishness b) an inadequate education c) paucity of imagination d) certainly all of the above. As if *to say* Kafka were *to be* him, cheap metamorphism.

But then again: after the reading, all I have is the name. Loss of text, disjunction from god. I recover by the sign of the cross: to say *en el nombre del Padre* as the shortcut of adoration.

Recuperation is here, in mere utterance of name: brief recovery of text, reader's brief sanctification.

Amorous indiscretion. Such volubility, such blatance of love, untiring discourse about books, at dinner tables, shopping centers, classrooms, séances, airports, beaches, toilets, museums, libraries, pubhouses, seawalls, conference rooms, studios, plazas, sports stadiums, fortunetelling sessions, hamburger stalls, salas, kitchens, bedrooms, bedrooms, bedrooms. Gush, gush, sputter, sputter, talk about books. Like a little girl without experience, unable to keep love from her lips.

Enamoration by language necessitates ejaculation by language. Conversation about books is the bibliolept's elementary form of satisfaction. But since bibliolepsy is always latent, seething beneath all activity, its emissions are continual, irrepressible. Places and events then just seem opportunity for biblioleptic expression, occasion for biblioleptic attack. The whole world is a stage for bibliovular release.

Lack of discrimination. The tendency to judge the writer only by successes, to excuse the badly written work. And finally, to love the bad book, the imperfect text, as much as the success.

The bibliolept is disarmed by failures of the text: not tolerant, as in that whore you want who expects all kinds, or charitable, like the mothering face of the virgin you want because she knows no better; but disarmed like the soldier who has pierced his opponent's flesh, seen blood run through a rupture. The imperfect text betrays to me my writer's mortality, weakening me, to lead me to a perverse pleasure. I begin looking for blood. I begin to smell beneath the lacquered text the honest skin of earlier failure. I track in the success the fractures of my writer's past. I hunt for his weaknesses, so that to find the scratch beneath, the indecisions and revisions, to find him in the raw becomes another adventure, equally vital, equally doomed.

Adulterous adulation. Such wanton superlatives, polygamous praise—the reader's capacity for adulation embraces a harem of texts, each pronounced "adorable." Is such dissipation of love moral? Is it healthy? Is it just, to declare Sylvia Plath "lovable" and Shakespeare equally so?

These superlatives rush forth spontaneously, and this spontaneity is the reader's integrity. It is one's escape from rhetoric, escape from the divisive rationality that will certainly, in a few minutes, cut up the text into the categories of one's prejudice, park it into its pigeonhole; but for a while, to merely exclaim (the way Barthes's lover exclaims) "Adorable": this is the reader's primal lucidity.

3. Dolphins

I am not one of your pathetic women with domesticated reasons for their "looseness" (a word with interestingly set parameters of meaning, even in the current century); I do not lay about so voluminously out of a homemade Freudian angst, although a friend of mine, over coffee and cockroaches in Diliman, has asked me:

were you ever beaten as a child? And I marvel again at the linear
meanings the word Freud has spawned, even in intelligent minds.
Nor have I copiously coupled out of an inherent female faithlessness, my incorrigibly indiscriminate cunt: at heart, I'm the most
faithful of creatures.

It might disappoint some people to know I had a happy childhood. I spent the first eight years of it with my father, Prospero
Peregrino, an animator, my mother, Prima, an amateur taxidermist, and Anna, my sister, a sort of witch. I was named after my
mother but have always been called Primi. Up until the time I was
eight, I traveled with them, spending my earliest years looking at
green and blue dolphins trailing boats in the sea. My sister Anna,
who is always seven years older than I and has treated me often
with the impatience my inability to catch up with her deserves,
has told me there are no dolphins in or around the San Juanico
Strait, in or near the Philippine seas, and I was too young and
stupid anyway to remember anything.

We lived intermittently in Tacloban, the capital of the Eastern
Visayan province of Leyte, typhoon path, lush place of impeccable monotony, a richness sworn to stasis of coconut green and
coconut brown and coconut white and yellow, living nightmare
of my sister, but to that we will digress in another chapter. For
me, things were different. The attraction was not Tacloban but
the boat travels we took to and from the city. We often traveled
in inter-island boats plodding through the Visayan provinces,
Cebu with its sparkling fish, Negros and its giant dogs, then

finally Mindoro's faunal feast: monkey-eating eagles; fabled bovine tamaraws; soft red-eyed tamarins, the smallest monkeys in the world; and dolphins like flashing glass domes, quick and thickly crystalline.

I think it was the dolphins that made my parents leave the side of the ship when I was eight. My father was a short man, eyes myopic and uncompromisingly sad. I see his eyes in the faces of many people, those destitute creatures, for instance, who stare at you asking for money, as if tatting on you guilt for their misery. I think the fierce sadness in my father's eyes, though, was basically his myopia. He was the only man in this country who loved his wife.

My mother was a beautiful woman, but she was crazy. She was descended on both sides of her family from feudal plunderers, on her father's side American, on her mother's side Spanish. My sister Anna is supposed to look like her—a plaster fairness of skin, moist like a new sculpture; a face like the mask of an ancient doomed prophetess. And underneath the stilled art of their features there was a dormant color, a sort of fire stirring in my sister's blood that made her flesh never static, never mere slab of stone. You see that in many women of mixed, infernal blood, I think, a reddening beneath eyebrows especially, around the ears and by the ankles, along the wrists and the nipples of the breasts and possibly above their pubic softness; at strategic points in their body: a glow. I shall always be sallow beside them. Contrary to all your expectations, I am not dark-skinned, dark-eyed, dark-haired. I'm not thin, slightly anemic-looking, I do not have hair that falls straight like a fan to cover my face. I do not have a voice that is part whisper, part preparation for a scream. What I got from my mother was her inclination to fat and a diluted form of her whiteness. My whiteness has none of the subtle passion of her hue; my skin has the tendency to turn the color of sour milk. What is interesting about my breasts is not a pale transparency that echoes blood, but a black birthmark near my right nipple, like a spider. My hair is an obvious light brown, and it curls naturally at the sides, only slightly, as if in a kind of forgetfulness. They say I have my father's eyes, but in pictures and in the light, the iris turns into a redness, wine-like, the way my mother's did.

My mother, as I said, was crazy. They say she couldn't stay in one place for more than four days—an exaggeration. My father, I think, was essentially sedentary (despite his name); you note that in his pictures, by his cheekbones that make him look Chinese, which he was: this immobility. He looks as if he would have wanted to stay in one house only for the rest of his life, making his cartoons. Instead, my mother took him along on her dead-animal trips. In the diary of their stay in Mindoro, one of the last places they visited, she said she wished to "find the one death that did not, in secret, wish for resurrection." Yet she was pleased to reconstruct the dead, keeping them alive with no effort. "The Authentic Resister," she noted in her diary, "is in none of these known animals. In my hands they all keep wishing to come back." My father, at the time, was on his way to making a full catalog of all the possible movements of the mouth, a philosophical undertaking as well as a practical guide for his colleagues. He already had versions of the coital and post-coital mouths and was in the midst of finishing that point at which the lips open ever so slightly, in either deep sleep or first lust. Anna and I used to keep these drafts with us, until by momentum of our disjunct lives we lost some, most probably in one of those flash floods Manila keels on as it weighs itself mindless into the sea. My memory tells me I was looking at those drafts on the boat that day, but, as Anna says, maybe I was too young and stupid to remember anything.

Aside from the drafts, my father also made drawings of unhuman men for commercial firms in Manila; he mailed them periodically in big plastic envelopes: coffins, he called them. My mother, on the other hand, was beginning to despair of anyone's ever really dying. In a tidy manner of putting it, my father the animator and my mother the taxidermist jumped off on the twin ends of these illusions—my father's productions of impossible lives and my mother's belief in impossible death; and there they are in the sea with my impossible dolphins. Among my father's effects that I still have is that unfinished mouth, which seems to promise so much in joy, the possible attitude of their first thrill as they looked together at the sea, at death that was, I suppose, another matter of lust.

"Beggars," Anna said. "Child beggars. Those are what you saw by the side of the ship. Children in the water yelling at us to toss them coins to dive for and keep. Not dolphins, ninny. Or I, too, should have seen them."

For six hours, the ship circled the waters. Divers jumped in pairs to look for my mother and father. They found neither. Prospero and Prima were last seen by a passing drunk, startled sober by flailing legs. Anna and I were in our cabin. People surrounded us to comfort us, as if the claustrophobia of bodies might help. Anna pushed them away politely by merely turning her back and bowing her head at the sea.

We were used to people crowding around us. When we visited my grandmother's towns, children followed us without compunction. Maybe because I was abnormally fair, albino-like (unless I put on my favorite rouge), and my sister was preternaturally beautiful. Also, we liked to speak in English, the language of my grandfather whom we never knew, a raspy, unreasonable proclivity. Such commotion over my family I took as a matter of course; and on the ship I believed, at first, that people were mistaken, my parents were merely up to one of their tricks—they liked to shock. Once, outside of a church, they had staged a mock mass with incompletely stuffed birds, one bird's head veiled by thin, flapping skin as if for church, an impressive eagle playing priest, dead birds snoring and birds with eyes poked out staring vacant and bloody. Kneeling at my pew I was horrified and didn't take communion, to expiate for my parents' folly. Anna was beside me, laughing. They did crude things like that. Also, my parents were very good swimmers. We lived by the beach, and they were always going off by themselves, at one point not returning until past the curfew hour, bedeviling us.

But the diving was in vain, and maybe I whimpered silently, without tears, because tears were not a Peregrino predilection; worse, my mother frowned on them. The dolphins appeared like silver floating rooftops, glinting and fatidic. The ship's motor roared and we headed home.

My mother's mother, the Abuelita, grand old hag drooling diamonds and saliva, was on hand to meet us when the ship docked. In the shock of having such suddenly orphaned grandchildren, she spoke to us in English when we stepped down from the boat. She usually spoke in a speedy and malarial kind of Spanish, I think to scare us. She was especially overwhelmed by my trembling wan eight-year-oldness and in a fit of sympathy deeded us instantly (she always had a lawyer nearby, half-man, half-beast) five barrios in Barugo and the plaza in Alang-Alang, which the municipal hall rented from her for use during fiestas and other affairs, and for which they paid her a fortune when they wished to install, in order to be like all other normal towns, a statue of Jose Rizal, even though no one loved him.

A new life began when I was eight. In this way my story is easy: it's so cleanly demarcated.

4. A bibliolept's father

My father was a Peregrino from Tacloban, the city proper, of Calle Veteranos, formerly Imelda Avenue, whitewashed and paved. When with the new regime it was given back its old name, it became again an avenue of decay, just like the rest of the city.

It's clear that progress is only a matter of fashion in my hometown.

My father's initial homestead remains the same, a plywood and beamed second-floor, one-room apartment, rented to his widowed Chinese mother by a Filipino landlord out of sympathy and inertia. Prospero was the son of a municipal clerk who died young and a half-Chinese woman who knew the guile of money but did not master its seductions: she was a two-bit usurer and visionary, compulsive mahjong player. His mother, legend tells it, died in the midst of taking a pair of winds to complete a mahjong of bamboo *escalera*: the symmetry of play knocked her heart out, and she expired ecstatic on the tiles.

My father struck out on his own. As a boy, he worked as a janitor at the Divine Word Missionary School to earn his tuition. A priest discovered his talent at drawing when the young artist drew, with delicate accuracy, the carabao nostrils and ovine hair of the priest who was to become the first Filipino president of the school in 1976. The priest who discovered him, a German, laughed outright but didn't even compliment the boy: he reprimanded him. Prospero soon left for Manila to learn the tricks of komiks drawing, then of animation, through vagabond passion and lucky breaks. His first big break was the war.

He was only seventeen and Manila was already an old city. Ruin was immanent in the usual places, the esteros of Chinatown, the view by the Bay, the circular plazas of Intramuros near which the stalls of whores and book dealers were to rise side by side. But there were already komiks, made of worse-than-toilet paper, which was convenient anyway for use in open-air bathrooms above the Pasig River. He hung around Tondo, hangout of romance komiks writers as well as of the vicious city hoodlums soon to fill the ranks of both traitors and guerrillas.

Amid Tondo's cynicism, the cunning of its cul-de-sacs and passion, my father learned the trade of wartime errantry and art from Dominador Velazquez Goya, dean of sensationalists and son of thugs. Goya, of full Chinese descent, like many of his conjuring blood in places that have erased them, had remade himself at the donning of a well-worn, famous name.

These notes I cull from random sources, but mostly from my godfather Diego Bastardo. My father never had anything to say for himself: he had the sullenness of people who are too easily moved. He had two obsessions: his cartoons and my mother. He let other facts be.

Here are some details I've managed to gather. Trained at first in sign-lettering, this Chinese tycoon Dominador Velazquez Goya soon saw where the money was in the printed press: the sentimo-singko komiks Manila devoured by the swarm, sold on sidewalks beside shoeshine boys and fruit vendors, featuring ornate stories of fatal love, bad faith, and stupid twists of plot—the diet of the Philippine siesta, if not of the Philippine soul. At the end of his life, Goya saw the renovations to his capital—rent-a-komiks benches before the gates of convent schools, blockbuster Tagalog films based on the engrossing silliness of his writers' plots—and the enterprising artist died content.

From a bedroom beset by the flavors of horsedung and the esteros, during the war Goya funded guerrillas and their enemies alike: "In business, like art," he told my young father, "one succeeds by a sense of proportion." Through Goya's connections, Prospero befriended radical satirists and collaborating illustrators. A quick study and silent autodidact, my father learned above all to treasure craft, the rigidities of light and dark, line and shadow, the deliberate temper of representation.

"He was blind to ideas," my godfather Diego Bastardo told me, "but alive to shapes, spaces, shades, like a dog in delirium."

His absorption with komiks drawing, the tidal wave of art as Dominador Velazquez Goya prophesied it, made him a lunatic among the imbeciles of Tondo in the forties.

In the fifties, in the exhumed gaiety of postwar dreams, my father's work was in demand among the burgeoning komiks houses of Goya's empire—action, fantasy, horror komiks, American-Japanese moro-moro komiks, in which Americans looked like Archangel Gabriel and the Japanese like bonsai Jack Palances, and above all romances, romances, romances. With sophistication in an industry come atomizing, categories, esoteric specialties. By the sixties my father was a whiz in all, drawing intricate monkey-men, Roman gladiators, Aztec gods, goat-redeemers, carabao clowns, harlequins, Byzantine courtiers, all the usual characters in the normal Filipino plot, and finally women: full-bodied, anatomically precise, naked. My father, I must admit, was a precursor of the "bomba" rage, salacious stories of carnal glee, though he was never a part of it. For my father, komiks' evolutionary slide into graphic passion was mainly a matter of technical precision, a lover's intimate erudition.

But who am I to know what went on in his possibly celibate soul?

I have no reports of amours, affairs, visits to whores, platonic interests, love rumors about him. I only know that in the late fifties, he was employed by a romance empire, and became famous for refusing to go "bomba," drawing women half-naked, breasts showing like swollen mangoes, when the story required simply a head and a balloon of words. For one piece, some late chivalry made him keep his women, with their snub-nosed profiles and deep, shadowy eyes, perfect bodies, and black lips, clothed in every frame.

"He was the only man fired because of his virtue," my mother once said of those days.

It was perhaps then that my father began what became known, in later, more sophisticated circles, as The Coitus Model Sheet, which he revisited and polished all his life. Imagine my father released from the bondage of other people's lusts and finding the pure lines of his own. Imagine him in postwar Manila configuring limbs and labia with both love and invention, a kind of fantasy of empiricism, precise and wild at the same time. A progressive friend who came from abroad saw his sheets of coupling couples, a series of pioneer drawings by this isolated man, and recommended him to the one of the animation houses in Asia, up north, perhaps in mutant, atomic Japan. He began to work freelance and piecemeal, practicing an art that for him had appeared in a vacuum—in the accidental space from which pure creation occurs.

This last is my own rumor, making its way into other documented allegations. What we know is that my father was one of the first to draw for companies overseas. They say that he visited Tokyo, and was so stricken by what he saw—progress and the wave of the future—that he began to draw what was known as his first real animator's scenes, *Velocity Man*. They were crude drawings at first, built from the heart's insular schooling—for all Filipino animators then had to teach themselves. He worked with a secret fraternity of men living before their time, working for the enemy: the future. It was a sect dabbling in pure art, because their work was conjured from almost nothing.

Viewers who might have the chance to watch the early versions of *Velocity Man* might note the special melancholy with which he drew the hero, who had the twin burdens of supernatural speed (his secret identity) and unspeakable illness (his ordinary life), the last of which made him irritable and prone to bad judgment. You might note the bitter look on his face when, in one segment, Velocity Man runs over a faithful, albeit misguided, admirer just to win a race: what purity of pain in those eyes, what subtle execution by the sad, tubercular animator, Prospero Peregrino.

For by that time my father had contracted TB; but much worse, he then proceeded to fall in love.

The difference between an animator and an illustrator, my father had once said to me, is that the animator looks only for the key to passion, while the illustrator crowds too many other things in his frame—he has not found his purpose.

To recuperate from his illness, he returned to Tacloban, a portfolio of in-between scenes to his credit, a freelance artist in a young business, with a contract to draw figures for an experimental cartoon for cigarettes: harbinger of "Champion sa lasa, Champion sa halaga": in short, he'd become a sophisticate. What a confusing thing life was that to the island he had left behind the woman he had been drawing in his old career as romance illustrator was herself returning, in flesh and blood, on the same ship as he. Two months later, they were married.

5. Love in third class

Prospero had never met Prima Mercader Watts in his life, but he recognized her kind from the start.

In the plots of komiks stories, women like her were obsessive compulsions, mortal dangers, and crosses to bear.

He could tell she wasn't used to the public inconvenience of the third class cots, with its fold-up beds squeezed together, the nylon cloth that served as mattress smelling of historical vomit and old sea air, the litter of banana leaves, chicken bones, and dried fish, and the blatant aroma of salted shrimp fry that went with every single meal eaten by a family of five in the cots beside her bed. She didn't even know how the cot opened and touched it only with the tips of her fingers, as if waiting on a magic word, *open kisame, abre-kama.*

My mother was returning from a convent high school in Manila. She was fifteen years old and soon to be impressed with the tall, lean artist, portfolio tucked under his arm who, in the beginning of the overbooked trip, had relinquished his cot to a mother and child and stood calmly by the railing, reading a book covered in brown paper.

"I thought he was a subversive," my mother said.

To girls in convent school, it was the mark of a subversive or a pervert to have a book covered in brown wrapper. Cocky college boys who illegally came calling on the girls, chiseling holes through gates or tipping the guards, might arrive with a nonchalantly pocketed book of unholy thinking in their back pocket, all the danger in their manner signified in the book's covered face. On the jeepney rides forbidden to the girls, a man in the front seat might have an opened, brown-wrapped book on his lap while he watched the ascent of every girl or woman onto the jeep. It was well known that men lived for these reflections. That's what jeepney mirrors were for.

My mother had never met a subversive. The silent reading man with long hair, thick sideburns, and broad and dangerous collar, which looked as if it could scrape a passing man's jugular, must be traveling third class by necessity. My mother thought: that was the rebel's fate—a vow of poverty and unease.

He thought she was beautiful but clumsy. It was too bad she was probably rich. He had learned to look at the beautiful women in the parties he attended with his friend, Diego the inker, bastard son a Cabinet official and itinerant seeker of beauty in the most inaccessible places, with the stoicness of Marcus Aurelius.

He had culled a hard philosophy from his random reading.

When he noticed her laughable way with the third class cot, he went up to her and opened it, put her bags on top of the bed, not under it as she thought she should: "You won't have much space to sleep on, but you can keep an eye on your things," he said in accented Tagalog. "Maybe keep your handbag under your knees." And he went back to his book.

Prima was traveling third class in defiance of her mother. She had been recently expelled from her convent school because of what were, to the nuns, sure signs of rebellion: cutting all her classes, except for biology, to ride jeeps around the city, missing Wednesday mass to read romance komiks in the library, creating origami animals that looked also like vulvas (they were cranes), collecting stray cats, and playing heretical music by sinful men, such as Paul Anka. She had an interest in zoology that alarmed the nuns. A declared blasphemer, a "bohemian," she had never in her life traveled with people such as these, a man whose luggage was a pig in a crate, a woman who opened her blouse to the world and suckled her pimpled baby, two old men talking about cock-fights and the schedule of pintakasi while they cradled crowing, brittle-beaked, actual live creatures within their arms. They ate with their hands and slept on their bags, and a young woman vomited vigorously and without shame on the floor then settled back peacefully onto her cot, the smell of her sick bagoong-balut-soda-and-rice lulling everyone to sleep. The man with the book was the only person she could trust in this teeming deck of wild and gloomy people who lived so freely with one another, their meals, breasts, dreams and vices open to every stranger like an unlidded and damp pot of rice.

Meanwhile, my father was beginning to feel the recuperative effect of the sea air, the provincial wind. The ship slipped Manila's harbor, and they were in the direction of no determinable place. Soon they were in the middle of a too vast world, and in this solitude of travel it was quite true that the Philippine islands were like dreams of each other, ideas unreconciled, lands not destined for discovery but, with luck, an apprehension. Magellan, Lapu-lapu, Maniwang-tiwang, de Goiti. Humabon, Gabriela, William Howard Taft, McKinley. No one had yet existed, not even the Negritos ranging like a colony of conqueror ants; and in the magic time between the glaciers and the gods there was a suspension of his country's fate. He was not required to live with confusion, silliness, despotism and waste, this balance between carnage and oblivion. The ship neared the province of Romblon, dangling in lunar light. As land darkened view, scope for speculation ended before he could even imagine a parallel life.

My father was refreshed by the jumble and roughness of the third-class deck. He felt a delayed nostalgia, a late sense of loss as he stood among his people—farmers with their gnawing animals; houseboys on vacation from flooded, sinking work in Manila, their beings crackling in four-inch platform heels and startling, luminous hair, pomade almost sentient, a separate life form; young women with fortunes sought and bartered, for which all they had to show were bottomless, endlessly replicating tins of M.Y. San cookies.

The younger people milled together late in the evening, comparing manicures and love affairs; men took out their cards and played blackjack and Eddie Peregrina, Elvis Presley of Manila, way until dawn. The older people—small-time merchants, an occasional rich miser who made her buck on usury and Marikina shoes sold on the installment plan—snored and slept or read the komiks of Prospero's young labors or about the goings on of movie actresses raped at fourteen in forty-inch type.

Prospero was happy in this crowd. He'd had no love to spare for the island when he'd been in Manila. To be in Manila, he had thought as a young boy, was like knowing the concept of life before all the frames were drawn. All the movies first came to Manila; the songs that gripped the country like seasonal dengue, the fashions that took hold of tardy provinces like well-used and ridiculous ex-queridas—all these began in the city he had left.

Manila to him had been the original plate; the rest of the country was mere impression.

But on the third-class deck, the wind blowing heavily from the weight of indirection, he saw with the clarity of a consumptive how fraudulent the attractions of Manila were, how mistaken was his pride. Manila was, in fact, a creation of the provinces, of the desperate or terminally optimistic provincianos of the third class, who fled to Manila in droves to seek their luck. Their intrepidity and nostalgia created the songs and fashions, the extravagance of sentiment and boldness of despair that ran Manila like the electronic system of a bomb.

So my father thought, thinking deeply on the instant. He had the wild turn of mind of a self-made philosopher. With the timidity of a philosopher, he kept to himself by the railing while my mother, fifteen-year-old Prima, switched on her orange transistor radio. It played the Platters and Brenda Lee, "Smoke Gets in Your Eyes" and "In the Mood"; but still my father didn't look her way.

It was late in the night. The roosters slept in men's arms, the tins of biscuits were all stowed. Prima woke to a pensive, prolonged rolling, a deep movement of the sea. She had struggled to get to sleep, summoning Elvis Presley tunes, the bones of the skeletal system, humerus, ulna, femur, patella, the clockwise order of the color wheel, yellow, green, and blue, *roy-g-biv, roy-g-biv,* the speeches her mother would screech in rapid-fire alternation between Spanish and Waray, the names of the seven seas, the capitals of the archipelago: shards of knowledge still polished and gleaming in the keen, unused cargo hold of her adolescent mind. She had lain still, sucked in her stomach to block the stench of the deck, and riveted her head to a rigid angle. She fell asleep finally, her radio softly crooning. Waking of a sudden, she raised her head, feeling the abruptness of her moving as if the gesture were liquid, a mobile mass, and she shuddered and cried—and vomited. She vomited loudly and bluntly on the wooden plank, spotting the hem of her sheet and a shoe's tongue. She smelled her sickness on her breath. Still people snored and the family beside her exhaled their salted dreams. As she lowered her head, instinctively, to liberate her larynx, esophagus, stomach, guts, a hand took her brow and the nape of her neck and held her steady, and again she spewed.

"Not for my music, my good looks, or my big silly eyes did he go near me," my mother said. "But for my vomit he came."

6. A brown-wrapped book

So the story goes: I was born of weak intestines and a brown-wrapped book. Their marriage lasted the span of my mother's life when she first met Prospero; a symmetrical life, in which beginning and end drew water.

In between there had been the squawking of the Abuelita and the literal heartbreak of my unknown Grandfather Watts: at his usurpation by a consumptive twice his daughter's age, Chinese to boot, he broke. He lasted only as long as it took to sign a new will, expurgating Prima's name, vilifying Prospero's. He was Leyte's druggist, but despite all remedies, grief and advanced ataxia took him on the morning of his daughter's wedding, a month after Prospero's birthday, with my sister Anna already plotting vagrancy and lust in her so recently pubescent mother's womb.

But all this is predictable, a common provincial chronicle. What interests me, of course, is the book. I keep wondering what Prospero was reading on that first boat journey. I imagine my father, shadowed and tubercular, profile deepened against water, reading the last poem Shelley had written before he died in the waters of La Spezia. Or maybe it was the passage in Melville, in which our archipelago is unnamed but recalled by the beckoning of a black vast sea, between the description of ropes and the listing of harpoons. Or a spill of commas from Jose Garcia Villa, riding the wind like sea-horse waves. Or perhaps it was the tale of his namesake Prospero, a betrayed man on a boat, laden only with books and a child.

"What was the book?" I used to bug my mother.

At four, I wanted details, hard facts.

"Oh, something. He picked it up in some stall on the Avenida somewhere, I suppose, so it could sit useless around the house."

"But what? Don't you remember?"

I remember my mother's favored attitude. Bending to pat stiff animal fur and, still bending, head tilted at an obtuse angle, eyes obliquely on the horizontal animal, she would stand contemplating a creature's bizarre, incipient resurrection, as if suspicious of its mortal intentions.

Like my father, my mother had chosen her own calling: the study of suitable modes of dying.

"Ay, puñeta, the bloodstains on this darned belly won't wash out, look."

My mom's interests, indicating a fetish for biological knowledge that did not become a woman, said the nuns in their final report, enveloped the house in an orgy of morbid smells and exclamations. I was used to the attitudes of disrepair: amputated bird legs, the soggy mess of primate brains, animals wired from neck to anus like clothes hung out to dry.

"How should I know what book it was, tata? It was such a long time ago. Besides, I was sick. I vomited my brains all over the ship."

With my father, it was useless. He never told stories about the past. He had no interest in it. He'd look up from his table, follow my mother's figure around like a cow after distant grass, walk over and catch her tummy from behind, or merely frown at his drawing and work on. It was up to me.

One morning, I opened all the house's cabinets to get at the brown-wrapped book. I looked into the mirrored and locked clothes closets, unused kitchen drawers, storage bins containing drawings of cockroach faces with varying expressions (*Anibal the Ipis, A Patriotic Cartoon,* my father's masterpiece, several years in the making), and the unlacquered, plywood-peeling space behind the giant glass comedor. Among my finds were: a pince-nez, two rusty scalpels, a pair of elegant, old-fashioned tweezers with talcum and hair congealed in dirt, secondary molars mummified in a silken stained handkerchief, the borax-dried leg and wing bones of some pigeons wrapped in cotton and blood, and two stiff, pointy bras made of rubber and stained lace. In the open kitchen, leaning against a firewall, stood a square aparador, with a mirrored door rust-pocked and water-eaten. It had been there for ages: the way my mother managed her household was by neglecting particular things. In there I found my cache: twenty-two brown-wrapped books stashed among lace ribbons untouched in their spools; a jar of glass eyes, opaque as death, for my mother's birds; yellowed chinos; Chantilly veils mothballed by Vatican II; and clean empty bottles of catsup and milk. There they were, thin books with a layer of dust building toward the girth of the book's thin pages. Several books opened automatically to the page where the spine was unglued, gaping and vulgar. I peeled the wrapper open: they were five-cent copies of Pocket Books, with the placid kangaroos on their spines, fairly rubbed out by the brown, flesh-like wrapper that had grown hair, a mat of follicles on its surface.

"I found it, Ma, I found it!" I rushed to my parents in the sala, clutching the books. "Which one of these is the book from the boat?"

I showed them my catch.

My mother looked up.

She stalked over and grabbed the books.

"Give them to me!" She was angry. "Where did you get these, maldita? Prospero, look!"

She waved the books at my father.

He gazed up from his catalog of extremities, robot hands and heads and elbows: "Prima, she's just a child. She has no understanding of those things."

"Not this child. She reads. Look!"

And my mother took my hand, brought me to my father, and held a book out to me.

"Primi, what does this say?"

"*Autobiography of a Louse.*"

"See!"

Triumphant, my mom shook the book before me, further damaging its spine and flinging borax dust in its wake. My father came forward. He pointed to a word.

"What about this, child. What does this say? And this?"

I read him the words *labia*, *mound*, and *fellatio*.

My father shook his head.

"She's a genius." He pointed to *fellatio*. "But what does this mean, tata?"

I shrugged.

"A kind of sea animal?" I ventured.

"See, Prima? She has no understanding." He pinched me on the mouth, smiling. "Tell your sister you don't need to be taught everything. Or your teachers will never like you." And he moved back to his lit table, contemplating evil in a casual stroke, magnificence and goodness in thick, sure lines.

My mother knelt before me with the book.

"What about this, Primi," she ventured. "What does this mean?"

"Lips," I said.

"Hm." She stood up. "You're right, Prospero. She has no understanding. But you're staying in your room until I say you can come out. No more spying on your mother and father. And give me those books."

7. I confronted my sister

Straightway I went up to the room I shared with Anna and confronted my sister.

"It's your fault. I'm grounded all day."

She was painting her toenails in extreme orange oils, using polish from bottles shoplifted weekly from Sen Po Ek Store.

"Little primitivity, what is it now?"

"They know I can read."

"Good. So now they'll stop lying to you about your stupid medicine being ice cream. It so clearly says it's medicine. Geez."

With the daintiest flick, Anna finished drawing the ear of a mouse onto her big toe and began to stab at the mouse's head to make a nose. Anna was a precocious body painter and budding miniaturist. She had our father's gift for forms, his swift fingers. At eleven, her dream was to learn tattooing and set up her own tattoo parlor.

"What's fellatio, Annie?"

"Spell it."

I did.

"Hm. Sounds like an illness to me. Wait. I'll check."

She lifted her toe and dragged herself by her heels and bottom to our set of the *Oxford English Dictionary*, leather-bound and gilt-edged, costing three hundred and twenty-seven dollars, not including postage and handling, the Abuelita said when she gave it to us as a Monday gift. On arbitrary Mondays the Abuelita, when she used to be sane, asked us to pick any object we wished and we could have it.

"Just to show you what you missed by the fact of your paternity," she rasped.

We used to ask for simple things, like boxes of Curly Tops chocolate or Bazooka bubblegum, out of respect for our impoverished father. But Anna once asked for a tamaraw hoof and got it. And although my mother immediately sent a note to the Abuelita to cease and desist, because she was despoiling the country's treasures out of malice and caprice, the hoof began an orgy of fabulous wishes: a civet's nail (which we didn't get: she gave us a tarsier paw instead), an autographed, limited-edition, cloth-bound oversized volume of my favorite book *Where the Wild Things Are,* and a talking puppet that recited *The Cat in the Hat* in three languages, depending on which string you pulled; the Spanish version was by the tail, the English by the gullet. It spoke French in a dusty slur through the white stripe on its furry hat. We ordered a twenty-volume set of the *Oxford English Dictionary* from a catalog when I turned four. When it arrived, it came with a pair of magnifying glasses, which Anna coveted and kept beside her bed, so she could use it to admire the monkey on her pinky nail or genitalia in *Gray's Anatomy.* She took the magnifying glasses as she looked for the word in volume V, *Dvandva to Follis.*

"Fatidicate, febricose, fecula, fell . . . there it is: fellatio." She looked at me. "Hm. Interesting."

"What does it say."

"'An act in which the partner's penis is sucked or licked.'"

"Yuck," I said. "Disgusting." Then I thought about it: "What's a penis?" I asked.

"'Hence fellator or fellatrix, the partner who performs such an act.'"

"What is it, a circus thing?"

"No, dummy. It's what people do when they grow up. Not even cats do it, I think. And *they* eat roaches." Anna returned to her toes. "Humans are pernicious," she concluded. She shoved the book at me and went on with her work.

I turned the volume around to look at the entry: every word was incomprehensible, except for the word sucker. But I liked looking at this book.

It had dates in it, a kind of biography of words. It listed down how words were used in different times, it wrote down sisters and fathers and cousins of words: it treated words like people with a personal history, the sentences like mysterious pasts you did not have to understand. They read like misbehaving ancestors. It impressed me then, that morning as I looked at the dates, that this word had been used in ancient times, 1887, what a long time ago, when people didn't have much to talk about most probably, and they thought about fellatio: the dictionary revealed to me times I will never know.

I looked up the volume for *penis*.

The mystery of the dictionary is a kind of foreshadowing of godly ways. You're looking for fellatio and find *feerie*: a phantasm, a faerie. You see feculence then februate: foulness and cleansing. One minute you come upon *febrient*, sickening of a fever, then next you find *frigorific*, causing cold. You find *fecifork*: "the anal fork on which the larva of *Cassida* carry their feces," and then you see incidental *feaze*: "to wear rough at the end." You look for *penis* and see *pipe*. You think that the world is designed, even in your random biblioleptic acts. But in fact, as in all cosmogonies, the construct breaks down. The page falls on coldly mysterious *dvandva*, "a grammatical term for a compound word, e.g., prince-consort" then next on miserably unlinkable *empennage*, the tail end of a plane.

You'll find, in the end, that it's not at all this type of design that makes you imagine some idle god might be leaning about your shoulder. Quite honestly, finding easy meanings in random acts suggests only a limited imagination (which may be an attribute of divine intervention). No, the wonder in the dictionary is the discovery of the possibilities of naming, that for any number of abstract or petty objects, thoughts or passions, one can find the right single term—from *telesthesia*, impression supposedly received from a distance without the normal operation of the senses, to *tits*, that organ of the senses with telesthetic design.

Contemplating this I think of the grandeur of god: not in pied beauties and dappled beings, but as a Dictionary of all possible multifold sensual things.

I found the word I sought and closed the book.

I left Anna to her art. Maybe I should follow my mother's advice, I thought as I left the room. She was right. Maybe I should stop reading.

It'll make you blind, my grandmother told me once when she caught me reading in my bedroom: "Reading at so young an age damages your vision. You'll end up like your father." She didn't impart her wisdom to my parents. She had washed her hands of all of us, she kept repeating every time she visited.

• • •

IT SEEMS STRANGE, but perhaps not: I don't remember learning. Anna had taught me, that much I know—but I don't remember her impatience or my stumbling through common surds, like the voiceless *L* in simple words, *would* or *could*. She tells me that when she taught me I'd skipped words when I wished, refusing to pronounce them—a basic nursery tale. I don't have too many memories except for these stories of childhood, of use only for retelling and important to none but those who remember—and sometimes, not even then.

You'd think that, going through layers of forgetfulness and its recuperations, I'd come upon some dim tableau of recognition. Maybe while laying the table or uncapping a pen, I should find a memory rustle back like a folding sheet of onion paper. Some startling clarity of recollection: one word, say, "body" or "tongue," transfigured from the mind's vague conception to a suddenly comprehensible, discovered word. But no such heavy-handed luck.

I do remember once, on a bus—I must only have begun reading with confidence—I got stuck on the words "Ini an Beer" on a poster. We were on the way to Alang-Alang, on unpaved roads that turned my stomach, and I fixed upon the poster as the bus hurtled past palms, carabaos, and liquid-eyed laboring people, who looked up at the bus, no matter how many routes they'd witnessed, as if the modern world were always a surprising interruption. I clung to the words "Ini an Beer," reversing them, inverting letters, rearranging, founding other colonies within them: Bern, Iran, Biñan. Moving from landscape to letters, words to world, I kept in my illness, alphabet-fixed; and with triumph, alighting at Alang-Alang, I stepped into the arms of the Abuelita—and tardily I spewed the spoils of my victory upon her chest. Like my mother, I had a weak constitution.

8. The Abuelita

My instruction in letters I blame, as did my mother, on my sister; but the crime of opportunity rests entirely with the Abuelita, my mother's surly mother who smelled always of lemon, a bitter and profuse scent that suitably announced her presence.

It may sound cold, but the use of the definite article for my grandmother was, in fact, a habit of the Waray language and did not so much indicate the pretension of titles but the laziness of our translation. "An imo Abuelita" she was and the Abuelita she remains. She was a Mercader from Mercader, a town on the southern end of the island that faced Cebu and the inter-Visayan waters, famed for the beauty of its women, the strength of its coconut wine, and the dramatic failure of its haciendas when the price of sugar began to drop. This tragedy warped even further the Hispanic humor and historically hypocritical nature of its landed class. They turned to percent borrowing on a grand scale, hastening their misfortunes, and they became enchained to the merchants who ruled the secret banks. They created the booming business Mercader was now famous for.

My grandmother was spared their agony: owner of back-breaking, ancient lands in Leyte, Cebu, and Mindanao, shareholder in those shipping lines that owned the boats roaming the Visayas in criminal states of decomposition, and upon his death heiress of unfortunate Grandfather Watts's string of pharmacies along lush coastal towns from Palo to Dulag to MacArthur, the Abuelita did well even when she sold her haciendas. A few hectares here and there were no sweat. Through the years, as her wealth increased in mindless predictability, her own mind diminished in proportionate fashion. That, too, was no surprise.

"Yours is just a town of usurers," my father would say to my mother, when Prima might begin some vague but extravagant harangue upon her exile in Prospero's Tacloban. My mother and father disagreed on a dozen sundry things. In that way they cemented their union.

"And your mother's not the worst of them," my father would continue, "which is saying much."

"Well, yours is a town of trivial peddlers and boatmen," my mother would say. She spent many hours looking out the window at the sea. The sullen pallor of her beauty was a regular sight for fishermen returning from a morning's catch. They would tip their straw hats at her from their slow bancas; my mother would nod back like a sovereign. She lived like them in a wooden hut in the grassy slums of Barangay San Jose, beyond the airport; but daily she greeted the morning with this measure of casual scorn. Her restiveness inspired respect among fisherfolk; her beauty offered a kind of love.

"A town abandoned by fate," my mother would pronounce. She had a litany of my city's dooms. "Magellan passed it by and docked at Limasawa. Martin de Goiti wouldn't even take its women. And General Douglas MacArthur—Tacloban's hero! He didn't even mention it in his memoirs. And after all that hoopla about his famous hoped-for landing, it's to this place he returned! What an anti-climax for the man.

"Even its patron saint abandoned this city. The Santo Niño left Tacloban to escape it, not to engender a miracle. Shame on Tacloban! It should have left the Holy Infant Jesus happy in Bohol or Bulacan or wherever it was the statue got lost in. He only wanted reprieve from boredom. Look at his face when we sing the final song at mass. *Santo Niño han Tacloban di ka namon igbubulag*. He looks as if he's about to shit from terror. He'll never be able to escape the Taclobanon.

"And Tacloban—what's the word it comes from? *Taclob*. To cover; hide. Ssch. Born to be obscure."

"Unlike Mercader, a town of usurers and hypocrites," my father would say calmly. "Built upon the name of the man who killed Trotsky."

My father had a talent for finding obscure connections. His vagabond life in wartime Manila gave him an entry into a world of suspicious pamphlets and soapbox philosophy. He claimed that the Abuelita was connected to the Spanish mestizo who had killed Leon Trotsky in Mexico City, ruining Trotsky's prized garden of roses in the process and scattering his commune of peaceful birds. Prospero had read about it in the papers when he was just a kid in Manila: the cutting is in a folder, among many other curiosities he'd picked up and digested; and he remembered the name when he had first met the Abuelita.

"Get off my property" was all the Abuelita had said upon seeing the Chinese man with her daughter. He had offered to carry Prima's suitcase from the ship to the unfinished hotel, off the pier, that the Abuelita owned. Her mother had met them. Smelling of kalamansi and shrimp fry, the Abuelita had glared at him, as if ready to spit, and walked off, clutching her daughter by the upper arm, scattering someone's Texas chicks.

The above-mentioned Mexican Mercader, who lived a subsequent life of fame in Moscow, was a mysterious man whom some legends say traced his roots to Barcelona, to which the Abuelita's genealogist also traced her name. And even if there weren't any connection, which was likely, my father would say, to tease my mother: "Trotsky murderer!" It was an unsound but scathing correlation. Maybe my father really did believe that it was because of this connection with Leon Trotsky, an outsider in Mexico (an alien like him, Chinese in Tacloban), that Prospero never visited Mercader.

"It's not the Abuelita I dislike," he would say at dinner. "It's all the symbols she drags with her."

Just as the Abuelita didn't speak a word to him after that first greeting on the pier, so my family never once visited Mercader in my father's lifetime.

Still, we used to see the Abuelita on her visits to Tacloban. She had her own house, on the other side of the coastline, near the provincial hospital, but she insisted on establishing her presence in our hut, by the airport. Her visits were invariably disastrous.

Once she had arrived after a trip in which she had picked up gifts for Anna and me from cities in different parts of Asia. I remember in particular my made-in-Bangkok umbrella that had tongues sticking out all across its brim, expressing my thoughts at suitable times. She kept buying me strange books: for instance, readers from Indonesia, in a language so close to Waray that it possessed a hallucinatory familiarity, with which many things struck me when I was a child. Anna received all the paints and tattoo needles she wanted, wrapped with the art of secrecy in which the Japanese excelled: the needles were kept in a layered box of paper so fine one imagined birds had woven it from the skimpy tendrils of their saliva.

Despite this, the Abuelita was not welcome.

"Who's this? Villa? Who's that?" I remember my grandmother sniffing through my father's desk, reading his books. "Are my granddaughters to be tainted with Filipino books in the house?" Her Waray was impeccable, but when she spoke it, in bits, she used to prolong vowels and glide over liquid consonants as if that made the language more Castilian—so she'd take a full heartbeat,

for instance, to say "Filipino." My father would remain silent in
his room. When she was sane, she used to read to us, guttural in
her speech as if her throat had a magic obstruction—she loved her
voice.

I loved her gifts. Lazy in the mind, she acted by prejudice, so
that her gift giving often had the added pleasure of irrelevance—
her spells of random spite. She kept giving me books when she
saw I liked them, and they were all beautifully bound but foolish.
A gilt-edged storybook of operas, so that I knew the tragedy of
Lucia di Lamermoor but have never heard the music. Different
Reader's Digest Condensed Books in many typefaces and colored
covers: I have no idea what the actual adventure was in *Kon-Tiki*,
because *Reader's Digest* had condensed it to an admirable, spine-
less zero. Too young even to go to school, I read everything with
love and guilt.

For a long time, gifts affected me with that guilty pleasure
I would feel then, as I looked through the books the Abuelita
bought. Reading, for me, was a luxury that pained my father.
I used to have a cloth-bound book called *Abraham Lincoln's
World*, published in New York and bought in Hong Kong by
the Abuelita. It's one of those illustrated chronologies built on the
charming reverence of those scholars of quotidian arcana, some
lone, erudite soul who needed to get a life. I believe it was the
first book I loved with a memorable passion: I remember some
pictures even now. Detailing not only Lincoln's life but the intimate development of contemporaries like Victor Hugo, Emperor

Maximilian of Mexico, Jenny Lind, and Queen Victoria, whom the author warmly called Drina, for obscure, obviously knowledgeable reasons, the book engaged me for hours. Little Drina writing to her Beloved Uncle Leopold in Belgium, Commodore Perry opening up Japan, David Livingstone reaching China, and Karl Marx breaking the heart of his poor mother by uniting the workers of the world, all while Abe Lincoln ran heroically for the State Legislature of Illinois, though he had never spent an entire year in school. But later in this chronicle I had to burn the book, watching Drina scarify on my mournful bonfire and Eugenie, the empress who had stolen Napoleon from sad, plump Josephine, curl up in ashes in a bitter swoon.

My GRANDMOTHER LAST visited before I turned eight. I was in my room. I put away the newspaper the minute I heard a knock, but the Abuelita was quick—she was in before I could tuck the sheets away.

"Aha, little Primitiva. Here you are. *Mira*," she said. "Look what I have for you."

Her voice that afternoon was weirdly nasal and squeaky at the same time: like a bat with a cold.

She was smiling in the way that made me see her glinting gums, her conspiratorial grimace. She had small, gapped teeth, like those in zippers. She held in her hands an elaborately bound book, in a kind of vellum and gold. It looked like the book I had wanted: an illustrated version of *One Thousand and One Nights*.

But when I held it close, I saw it was something else. It was hard-bound and heavy, still wrapped in plastic.

"It's imported," she said. "You cannot find this even in Manila. They're fairy tales from India. The most expensive book among the smuggler's goods. I knew you'd want it. But you have to read only in the daytime, without candles, for ten minutes. Is that clear?"

She saw the newspaper in my hands.

"Are you reading about what happened?"

I shook my head.

"Don't lie. Give that to me. I'll tell you this, Prima—because your father won't."

She moved close to me and leaned over. She took the sheets of paper. Her back was stooped in a flexible curve. Her blouse shifted, and I could see her bones sticking out along her back—a ridge of knuckles. Her bony body looked like a collection of fists, hard edges and brittle jabs.

"*Ten cuidado*," she whispered to me. "She is throwing little children down bridges."

"Who?" I asked.

"Why, the First Lady, of course. Everyone knows that. And if your father doesn't stop sending those cartoons to the newspapers, you could be next. I'm going to find my little grandchildren in San Juanico Strait, both of them ghosts. You tell him that."

I heard my father's voice outside my room.

The Abuelita made a face.

At the door she put a finger to her lips, the newspaper dangling with her gesture.

"*Cuidado*," she said.

She left my room.

"What was she here for?" my father asked.

"My birthday present," I said to him, smiling. "Look."

I showed him the book.

"It's exactly what I wanted," I said. "A book of fairy tales."

The *Kama Sutra*, he read.

"You think too much of what you want, Primi," he said. "Try to think about what you do not need."

He moved as if to take the book from me; then he walked away, leaving me with my gift.

"Ignorant old woman," he muttered as he closed the door.

I believe it was with sadness that he would say bitter things.

It was my mother who took the book from me. She threw it in with the day's trash, with the monkey blood and clamshell leftovers. I cried in my room, but by then I had begun to adjust to my mother's wrath. I soon forgot about it.

Later that evening, they quarreled.

"It's her book, her gift. Anyway, she'll learn about those things one day," my father was saying. "She wouldn't have understood a single thing in the book, but she might have learned something of the beauty of the human body's design." My dad shrugged.

"Have you no concern, no sense of responsibility, Prospero?"

My mother was very thin in those days, almost as gaunt as

Anna, who was growing like an ogre, tall as a beanstalk. My mother Prima, on the other hand, looked as if she were being poisoned by formalin and borax. At rare times she'd be irritable with my father.

"Books are precious, Prima," he said softly, trying to persuade her. "It is wrong to throw them away. That's what I believe."

"But did you actually see the gift? It was fully illustrated, with big pictures and ugly scenes. It should have been confiscated immediately."

My father sighed. I imagined that he'd moved closer to my mother, holding her where he always touched her first: below her left breast, by her diaphragm. My father was a man of habit. "You're right, Prima. What do you think of this?"

I entered the room to find my mother looking at a cartoon.

It was another version of Anibal the Ipis, about a magic Filipino cockroach, which was never to see print.

"Oh, Prospero," my mother murmured. "You know what I think: politics never makes sense. Especially in cartoons."

I asked my father: "Why are they drowning children in San Juanico Strait?"

Prospero looked at me.

"Who told you that?" he said.

"The Abuelita."

It was then that my father got mad. He spoke to the world: "That's what you get from a convent education in Spanish. Arrogance and idiocy."

To me, he said: "There's a war in the country, Primi."

"Shut up, Prospero. There is no such thing."

"Yes, there is, Prima. You know it. There's a war in the country and that's why people are dying. It's not magic. There's a dictator who is consolidating his power by—"

Prima walked away from the room, her hands upon her ears. "Politics, politics, politics. It's ruining your mind."

LATER, MY FATHER was to figure in that famous tiff before the nation; but in a very peripheral way, of course. He was just a lowly animator. His drawings of Anibal the mystical cockroach went nowhere. He submitted many sheaves of it to a contest for a patriotic cartoon; it didn't win. But it had caught the eye of a company looking for cheap reproducers of a soon-to-be-famous cartoon. The elaborate, segmented geometry of my father's cockroach hero was perfectly suited to the robot images of the famous *Voltes V*, which he drew only in imitation, of course. He drew ink versions of the robots' compartmentalized bodies, so much like the precise anatomy of his entomological savant. The imitation robots of *Voltes V* engaged his fervor the way all other heroes had before them—Velocity Man and the bomba girls. But my sister Anna believed these robots were the sum of his pride.

"Those transformable creatures, recreating their own body parts in miraculous contortions—do you think that's what he wanted to be? A reversible, invertible, metamorphical roach? Our father was the über-Gregor Samsa, but in reverse: maybe it was he who wanted to be transformed? I'm sure there was something heroic in his death—we just can't tell what it is."

Anna told me this very early on; but I forgot about it in the excitement of the final episode of his professional life. Several years after Prospero died, the dictator banned the watching of *Voltes V* cartoons. Government had rejected his cockroach; now it had banished the last remnants of his shadowy art. Protests were called against this censorship. Young fans wrote angry letters. But the robots remained banned. I could only think of the implications of this turn of events—what my father would say. I knew what Prima would have answered: "Politics is ruining your mind."

THAT VISIT WAS the last time the Abuelita came to our hut. When I next saw her, she was at the pier, wailing. She was disheveled, almost blind from weeping when we came upon her. She had to be propped up by her lawyer, an unsavory yet recurring figure.

9. Atorni Sugba

Attorney Filomeno Sugba was the Abuelita's lawyer, also her genealogist, tarot card reader, and occasional driver. Atorni Sugba, as he was called, had a lean, scholarly face that came from his having had to take the bar four times. His story, as we knew it from the drivers and the maids, possessed an epic stupidity common in provincial tales: Juan Pusong of the legal trade, Bongbong Marcos of the bar. Studying law in his late thirties, he gained minor fame in his neighborhood for persevering at the bar exams when men of lesser character and greater self-perception gave up. Finally passing the exam, by a miracle of Saint Jude and the Holy Child, who rolled the dice in his favor in a moment of weakness they've since regretted daily, so the maids say, he promptly lost a case on his first day in court, because the fiscal failed to call him *Atorni Filomeno Sugba*, upon which Atorni Sugba punched him. He earned days in prison and an official reprimand from the Supreme Court. After Diego Bastardo, this man was the principal male in my life upon my father's death.

He had a glance as cunning as a cur's, always sidelong. He had an overbite and a weirdly gray face—especially around his mouth. At certain angles, he looked devolved, or like a creature in a fairy story, the Big Bad Wolf.

He was the man we leaned on during the time of the funerals.

10. The funerals

Anna and I had refused to attend the funerals of Prospero and Prima. At first, they were to be buried separately in one day, my father in Tacloban, my mother in Mercader, although we had not recovered their bodies. Still, the Abuelita had a couple of coffins constructed, of pure narra. My mother's was inlaid with mother-of-pearl, like a beautiful cabinet in which one might shelve numerous, paperbound books.

It was perhaps the extraordinary loneliness that this thought provoked—that we were to attend funerals for which even the dead would be absent—that set Anna on her hunger strike.

My father's coffin was to be buried first. My mother's was to be flown by rented helicopter to Mercader, which in those days was more than a day's car ride away from Tacloban. The Abuelita was elaborate in her grief: my mother was to be buried like a true Mercader, in ridiculous and wasteful pomp. And even in empty coffins, they were not to be blessed together.

But things happened. The helicopter pilot got sick; a sweet musty scent filled my mother's room in the Abuelita's house in Tacloban for no clear reason; and Anna staged her hunger strike for nine entire days, as if in imitation of a scene in the news.

Atorni Sugba stood by the door, carrying raw tamarind and salt on a plate: Anna's favorite fruit dish. It was the ninth day of her fast; the coffins were to be buried the next morning.

"Sige na, hija. Eat. They're not so green, not so soft: sour as you want them. Sige na: you might die, you know."

Anna didn't even shake her head. She didn't move. On the first day of her fast, she had said: "I shall not eat until the Abuelita says they will be buried together."

"Blackmail!" the Abuelita said.

She, too, would not give in.

The maids proceeded to offer Anna all the fruits they could get hold of: chicos, sineguelas, star apples, manzanitas, lanzones, papayas, atis, mangosteen, jackfruit, mangoes, pomelo, bitter, sweet, gummy, seedy, ripe, green, curled, fried. Anna was a legendary fruit lover. She even ate durian, whose shitlike smell she loved. Daily, Atorni Sugba brought food to her room. For those nine days, she took none of what she was given.

Today she didn't speak. I could smell her skin, rancid like old fruit peelings. Her breath was coming from her mouth, and it was noxious: fumes of sorrow smell simply like sick curdled spit. Anna lay on her bed in her posture of defiance, that is, spread-eagled like the Christ. But she had no expression now, not the snooty glare that clarified her pupils into gray nor the pout that relaxed into her mouth's usual sneer. I was getting worried. She had at first looked defiant. Now she seemed merely starving.

Atorni Sugba left the plate, slinking toward my grandmother's room.

I looked at my sister again. I brought the plate to her side.

"You have to eat, Anna," I said. "You're beginning to get wrinkled."

My sister stuck her tongue out. Saliva webbed from her mouth in solid, cottony wisps. Then she turned away from me.

AT THE START, I had been extremely impressed and watched the proceedings with great interest while reading about an orphan. In the book, the mother dies while a big-bosomed, straight-talking, sweet lady comforts the orphaned boy. I remember most the kite the orphan flew in the beginning of the book. I could easily imagine I was in a field of buttercups, grieving amidst beauty while I waved a string in the air, my kite, my link to heaven, where dead people lived. But when I took up the book again, years later, once when I was idling in this bookshop, I could not find that scene with the kite, though I swear it was there.

I, too, didn't eat at first. But I also walked about and talked. I wandered around to see what the maids thought and what the funeral guests and kibitzers said. I listened to my grandmother's hysterics about the helicopter pilot's unfortunate angina. In short, my own fast didn't count for much. I was functioning normally, not even like a grieving child.

I heard the maids whisper about the thickening ghost smell in my mother's room.

"That could only be Señora Prima. If I had died like her, I would start haunting the world, too," Marga said as she picked chaff from the rice.

The fact of a ghost didn't scare or surprise me. But its manner of apparition did.

I walked into my mother's room again, to smell the delicious scent of her ghost in the air. It was quite a strong smell. A bludgeoning sweetness like decaying armfuls of sampaguitas. A pollen fatness. The strange thing was that my mother had never liked flowers. "They're much too alive," she always said. On her birthdays, my father would give her books about mammals or ichthyology.

I walked about the heavily floor-waxed, closed-up room, wondering why my mother chose flowers to represent her in death when she had never really liked them in life. The afterworld certainly changed a person, I thought. I stood there practicing my underwater breathing technique, a mindless hobby of mine. As I breathed in, the smell of flowers grew thicker.

I closed my eyes and remembered my mom in her happiest, most tranquil moments: when she was taking intestines out of dead monkeys, scooping them out with fond precision. Or when, chemically polluted and triumphant, she would present her newest finished product, a gigantic, garnished cicada—a toy, actually, merely requiring formalin—or some rare and ugly rat.

I breathed deep, trying to imagine what it had been like for my parents, submerged in water without air: it must have been awful, even if they'd been with the dolphins.

The smell in the room smothered one like an ocean.

Getting dizzy from the smell, I opened a window and looked out. By the window, it hit me with full force. I had to stop breathing. My mother's ghost was sitting on the windowsill. I thought: she had turned into a smell. But there it was on the branch among scraggly, long-fingered leaves. A fortune flower.

It was blooming with the fervor of penned grief; it was a signature of sorrow. The fortune plant's flower blooms once a year if it blooms at all. If it does, it blooms only in the night, when its yellow petals like stiff slender fake nails open up and emit a nauseous heady gloom. In the daytime it reverts to a dead pale blandness. Its petals turn brown like old hairs on a jackfruit. It looks like the wrinkled arm of a monkey too sick to be any good for stuffing. I saw what my mother's ghost was, and I fled the room.

"Abuelita!" I called out into the living room.

"Primi, bella!" An arm came around me, and I was smothered in the bear hug of my godfather, Diego Bastardo. He must have just arrived from Manila. I struggled out of his arms, and he looked as ugly as ever.

The maids said Diego was the spawn of witchcraft. His dark skin and the hump on his back made the maids snicker and make tales: they were put-upon women with the prejudices of the strong. He had been our household's only regular visitor when my parents had been alive.

I hugged his familiar bulk. His torso was built like a banca: there was a bony curvature in the back, and to embrace him you had to keep finding a comfortable angle, as if you were drowning.

"Uncle, I found my mother's ghost. Come and see. Abuelita, come and see."

The Abuelita had followed Uncle Diego into the room.

I showed them the fortune flower by the window, lolling from the tree like a feather duster.

Diego Bastardo took in the smell and sight and said, as if he were admonishing the plant:

"'I've bound your arms and hair with vine and bound you /
With wildflowers but you are crying still.'"

And he broke down by the window.

I'd always known Uncle Diego was a sentimental man: under-
developed in the roughness of the world.

With my father, he used to stagger around drunk reciting
poetry, badly sung lines from different poets.

"What?" was all I could say to him.

"Luis G. Dato," Uncle Diego said, turning to face me. "Your
father never liked his poems."

The Abuelita took in the figure of my godfather, his short, low
legs that made him look like a starved goat, his easy tears. She
disliked him.

His grief was an affront to her own.

"I'll tell them to air this place more thoroughly," said the
Abuelita, and she took my hand and led me from the room.

The next day, my sister failed to wake up in the morning. She
was sent to the hospital, and the funerals were called off.

Anna's lips were crumpled like paper and her face needed ink.
She was whiter than the ghost I had imagined my mother to be.
At the hospital, Anna continued to refuse all water, rice, or fruit.
They stuck a needle in her, and I waited for her face to refill, like
Orange Sunta in a straw. It didn't.

I thought: maybe Atorni Sugba was right. Maybe she will die.
I looked into my book to see what the orphan was doing. I was
beginning to be quite interested in the relationship between the

coach driver and the sweet-talking, big-bosomed lady. "Barkis, ma'am, Barkis is willin'." When the lady married the coachman, I was sure she would abandon the orphan child to his cruel fate.

Unlike Anna, I had eaten breakfast daily once they began putting pancakes and chicos at the foot of my bed every morning. I ate the balimbing she didn't eat, and I ate the guavas and papayas. I was getting fat. I had gained weight on all kinds of Anna's favorite fruit while she petrified in bed.

And while I ate I read, devouring the many twists and turns in the life of the orphan, imagining I was the girl he was to marry, and then realizing I had no wish to be like her: she was sickly. It was very clear that soon she was going to die.

Protein degradation, secondary skin infection, inanition, epigastritis. My sister was pronounced sick of everything.

"Her depression could relapse any day," the doctor said.

I read aloud pages from the book at random while the fluid dripped into her wrist like white blood.

"'I was not sorry to go,'" I read to Anna. I propped the book against the bed, close by her. "'I had lapsed into a stupid state; but I was recovering a little and looking forward to Steerforth . . . Again Mr. Barkis appeared at the gate, and again Miss Murdstone in her warning voice said 'Clara!' when my mother bent over me to bid me farewell.'"

My voice acquired confidence. I was getting into the spirit of the thing: "'I kissed her and my baby brother and was very sorry then; but not sorry to go away, for the gulf between us was there, and the parting was there, everyday. And it is not so much the embrace she gave me that lives in my mind, though it was as fervent as could be, as what followed the embrace.

"'I was in the carrier's cart when I heard her calling to me. I looked out, and she looked at the garden gate alone, holding her baby up in her arms for me to see. It was cold still weather; and not a hair on her head, not a fold in her dress, was stirred, as she looked intently at me, holding up her child.'"

Silence: that's all there was. Then I heard it.

"Well, go on. Get on with it."

I looked across from the book—Anna was wide awake.

She had always been impatient with emotional scenes in books.

"Well, what are you waiting for? Go on with that loser's life."

I rang for the nurses.

Anna was tugging at her needles.

"Read on," she said impatiently. "What comes next?"

I didn't kiss Anna, but I read happily.

"'So I lost her. So I saw her afterwards, in my sleep at school— a silent presence near my bed—looking at me with the same intent face—holding up her baby in her arms.'"

ANNA WAS SOON on liquids then on mashed goo. Her skin stretched, her color stabilized from wan newsprint to linen bond. She had a manicure, and her toes were repainted to a plain blue hue. So swiftly out of Dickens and into the fake regularity of life.

In the end, Anna and I both refused to go to our parents' funerals. The ceremony happened without us. I suppose their empty coffins are there still, on Tacloban's cemetery hill in El Reposo, facing the sea in separate graves. But Anna got her way. They were buried in the churchyard together. I've never gone to see those graves: I keep thinking I'm too fat.

One sad sidebar was that, spurred by a momentarily dense sense of tragedy, Anna and I burnt gifts the Abuelita had given us: in memory of Prospero. It was a weak moment. The pyre itself was pathetic, as it was part of the garbage dump in the back of our grandmother's yard, fuming already with ugly wastes, fishbones and things, that were quite irrelevant to our sorrow. I regret the books especially; I saved only one volume, part of a dictionary, *Dvandva to Follis*.

11. The library of Alang-Alang

When Anna was well, we were deposited in Alang-Alang, where we were to live in my grandmother's house, while the Abuelita spent her days traveling about the provinces, muttering increasingly to herself as she cast about in her unhappy world. It's said that in the end she had a lover of seventeen to whom she gave the remains of her haciendas and a bunch of large blue sapphires. But the stories are so much like komiks—one is hard put to make anything of them. We rarely saw her. We reminded her of Prima,

I suppose, especially Anna; her sorrow over her daughter stulti-
fied further her already weak head. She left us to ourselves.

I liked the name Alang-Alang. What kind of townspeople
would name their town after a prepositional phrase, I thought,
or a verb? In Tagalog, alang-alang means "in memory of." In
Waray it means to hesitate, or stumble along. It meant two
things, and I was always unsure which to choose. On the journey
to Alang-Alang after Anna was discharged, Anna and I were in
the back seat, Uncle Diego was in front. Atorni Sugba drove. The
Abuelita waved goodbye to all of us, though at that point, it was
not clear whether she recognized anyone: she was drunk on tuba
and soaked in grief, a near-fatal combination.

What I most dislike about car rides is that I can't read. As
a child, I used to try, but then my brain would lurch, and I'd
vomit. Now I just sit and stare at far-off hills or telephone lines.
I once read in a magazine article that there's a nerve in the head
the main job of which is to allow a person to read in a moving
vehicle. It's like a signal, a release button or a lever. It permits the
reader to separate the words in the book from the moving world
before her. Otherwise, the brain receives the words as if they, too,
were in motion, unstable and liable to hurtle down a cliff.

I don't have that signal: before my eyes, words and world sway
and start, slide and sputter as I read in a car. I make an effort to
keep the text still, but my mind gives way, and the words trundle
along with the scenery, slapdash as the mountains. Life, then, is
inseparable from language, brain blends with moving book—I

have no lever in me that separates text from the living world. It's a simple medical matter, motion sickness, but one might also consider certain infirmities to be a kind of sign.

ON THE WAY to the house, I felt sick, so we stopped to drink some orange soda in front of the Municipal Elementary School: Ang Mababang Paaralan ng Alang-Alang. The Squat, Lower School of Hesitation. Atorni Sugba and I left the car. Anna and Diego stayed behind, reading my father's juvenilia, old komiks stories, which Diego was giving to us as a parting gift. He was leaving the next day for Manila, where one of his starlets was peeing in her pants over some wild controversy or another: virginity by hearsay or some such bad luck. In the middle of his life, Uncle Diego had achieved a position suited to his temperament—as manager of actresses in various stages of distemper. They were all flighty, undependable beauties with whom Uncle Diego would fall periodically in love, with the mad habit of an aging, excessively gentle, hopeless man.

I think often of Uncle Diego. That maybe if we had accepted his offer to fly with him to his home (he had gained a small bit of inheritance from his politician father) right then and there, we wouldn't have wasted our time on the quests for shelter that we did undertake. We would have had a steady refuge in Uncle Diego.

Instead, we continued our trip to Alang-Alang.

Because I needed to pee, Atorni Sugba unlocked the thick,

rough-hewn door of an unpainted building. The door was heavy as a convent's. The building itself, roundish and made of stone, looked like a badly done belfry, smelling moistly of excrement or sin. The Alang-Alang Municipal Elementary School Library was called "Aklatang Doña Gregoria Mercader Watts," which was declared in rusted brass, the only metallic ornament of the room. In it were shelves of beautifully bound books. The room smelled of cured goats and dust, the aroma of old leather and wood caged in stuffy neglect, of mold and damp goods. On the shelves were books donated by the Abuelita and other usurers, their names etched on the chairs. It had the best books of all—the romances of Sir Walter Scott and Winnie the Pooh; the lives of Bambi the deer and Plutarch's Greeks; Bobbsey twin adventures and the life of Tristram Shandy; *Sonnets to Orpheus* and Sherlock Holmes; the Justice League of America and *Thus Spake Zarathustra*; Betty and Veronica, and Emily, Charlotte, and Anne. In a glass box in the center was a huge facsimile folio of what looked like Shakespearean plays, imported from England and bound in calf because the Abuelita was a snob. Side by side Shakespeare's misspelling of his name was the larger signature of my grandmother: DONATED BY, it said discreetly.

Here I was to spend the rest of my childhood, a space in the mind rolled up like an old carpet, and if you unfurled it, all you'd have would be random sensations of place. Leather, pulp, the cacography of lovers etched on a table: "Mheena luvs Jhon," a termite-eaten stub, an armrest in which the devouring animals managed to prefigure, strangely, what could be the whorl of someone's wet, page-turning thumb. I'd stay in this room after school—I owned a set of its keys; and I remember the spot where, at twelve, I found I could quite naturally become an instant fancied suicide, so strong was the hold of certain phrases on a newly menstruating girl. In here I progressed from various obsessive compunctions, trapping grasshoppers in encyclopedias or tasting in secret the fat black ants on a spine, and the minutiae of childish challenges—mystery books and crossword puzzles, acrostics and anagrams. I believe the library buildings are still around, functioning mainly as a dance hall, as the town grew in prosperity and indulgence. The land behind the buildings, though, is forsaken, I've been told—a reputation of ghosts, bolstered by a mystic number of jeep accidents along that stretch of road, has cursed it, and so the land remains lush, while the books have been slowly deleted, trashed, to make room for microphones and karaoke, all the seasonal paraphernalia of small-town dances: plastic chairs, skirted tables. The dark grass outdoors is conducive to what must go on besides the music, distinguishing dancer from the dance.

On that morning, I stood before the case of massive books, breathing in the smell of stuffy, dense pulp.

Atorni Sugba came up to me while I was looking at the case.

"Let me wipe your clothes," he said to me.

I turned toward him, but my hand moved to lift the glass lid.

"Can I touch them?" I asked. The case's lock was open and the lid was easy to lift. I reached for the book.

He was busy brushing at my blouse, rubbing the spit off my shoulders. I stood still. He started rubbing against my chest, my nipples.

"Can I touch this?" he asked, moving his head down to my face.

Against my chest he had pressed his hands. His breathing and mouth, gross as a goosequill, ugly, gristly and wet, scribbled dank ink on my face. I lifted the book, and the porous parchment of the heavy book met the man's sweaty mass. The book was an ungainly shield. I finally heaved the folio against him, in a burst of energy I can't quite see, and he fell against a thick, grade-school chair. I ran out of the room through the open door. Anna's legs were stretched outside the car, bare and pale. Diego was drawing on them some quick cartoon sketches.

"Hi," Anna hailed cheerily. Unwrinkled now, she was still too pale. But her cheeks were flushed and at that moment she looked almost happy. "Ready to go?"

Through the rest of the drive, I held in my pee and my story, while Anna relayed the stories Diego Bastardo remembered about my father, with Diego chortling occasionally at the legends he told so well.

12. Do not imagine

Do not imagine that the folio of plays in the glass case contained *The Tempest*, featuring Caliban and Miranda, who had a dying father named Prospero. The girl, I imagine, became a bookworm at the death of her father. After all, he had been wizard of books, which, you might say, became her own form of Ariel—Prospero-less on an island, she had to make do with the sprite of words, the airy immortality of texts.

No, no, it was no such thing. The folio was a book of histories, those Henrys and Richards, now unaccounted for, traded for the karaoke.

13. A bibliolept's admission

In fact, should I even go as far as to say that it may not have happened that way? That I have the act and outrage right, but maybe not the time and place? I might admit that it occurred in our living room in Alang-Alang, in warm daylight with the sun outside fairly chirping with brightness. I could say that he had pecked me on the cheek in the open air, and then he had taken me to his chest, leaning against my nipples like a taut tree trunk on a windy day. That I had simply scampered away, completely textless and surprised.

It's not much of a bibliolept's story, told in this way. It absolves my life of heavy-handed exposition. Which is a good thing. To clear me of that narrative crime, I am tempted even now to own that it was not so, it did not happen in a library. But it's my misfortune that I cannot revise my past.

In this case it is a strange history of events trailed by a track of books, like that path of bread crumbs leading lost children home, in those nursery tales I used to read a long time ago.

14. Boat-setting days

Boat-setting days weren't over after Anna and I settled at Alang-Alang, Northern Leyte. Early in the school year, Anna was pulling me out of class every few weeks, bringing me to places according to fruit season, Talisay, Cebu, when the chicos were ripe, Guimaras for the mangoes. And as I learned some more geography, she took me to Bohol when the chocolate hills were green and Batangas when the tide was red. Crisscross around the country, dissipating the earnings of two of the barrios, while my sister's look of foreignness and smell-of-fruit snared men in different places. She herself dropped out of school, like Abraham Lincoln, having an energy much too extravagant for it. Talk of school and she'd spit, a literate enough gesture. She was supposed to be applying to colleges, but instead she waited around while I went through fifth grade and sixth. In the meantime Anna went through men, pakwan-men from Palawan, rambutan from Romblon, splitting seeds and leaving shells, feeding like a rodent-scientist on various pulpy rinds. Such was the power of owning the municipal plaza and several small barangays that the local elementary school of Alang-Alang allowed me to go in and out without fuss, managing to graduate me grade-school valedic-torian as well, an honor I also owed to my increasingly biblidiotic habit—reading with rapacity and monomania, lying antisocial and inert.

On the boat rides I had spent with my parents, on the wind of my sister's vast boredom, there had been nothing much else to do. Memories of my childhood run before me as synchronized dichotomics of places and books: *Les Misérables* and Leyte, Aparri and Apollinaire, Cavite and *Cavalleria Rusticana* in a yellowing book of opera, passion made stark being music-less. I threw up in car rides, but on boats my mind was on even keel. My horde was eclectic, opportunistic. I held on to my favorite history book, though I could not read it, *The Price of Freedom* by General Jose Alejandrino, while we drove the ancient rail route from Manila to Dagupan, my sister in the back seat with egregiously decorated future husband Joaquin Valenzuela, whom I imagined to be the grandchild of Don Pio Valenzuela, an obscure Filipino patriot who sadly betrayed the hero, Doctor Jose Rizal. On that day Joa-quin wore plaid bell-bottom double knits and a rock-n-roll chain on his neck.

Unknown to the Dagupan road, in the future I was to live with my sister and Joaquin for exactly three years, through the inevitability of floods and my sister's ineluctable leaving: in a house cramped by his refusal to use my sister's money, one toilet and no view, two bedrooms with a poster each, one of Kafka, the other of Groucho Marx, books spilling from the uncarpeted sala to the kitchen and beds, four uncarved wooden chairs, no fruit trees—hardly any room for my sister's screams. Poet of a lexical insomnia, pulling incessantly at the nerves of words, Joaquin was the only man my sister was to marry and the thirteenth man whose heart she broke. When I first met him he was wearing a silver icon that meant Peace.

15. Now let me cite other biblioleptic scenes

A) The year I turned twelve. I was on the stairs leading to the Abuelita's house in Mercader. I could see the river that ran through the town and smelled sweet in summer, like a basket of live fresh fish. But the river wasn't clear now, or sweet, and the house was crowded like a fiesta. The mango trees were thick and dark and fruitless, and my solitude hummed in me like a river. The Abuelita was dead. I held the book in my hand and her body lay like the Queen of Egypt in the house. Candles from France and flowers from Barcelona and the Vice-Consul to Spain who was her seventh cousin creaking around in his giant white shoes, hair smelling like bad fish. All the rich ladies with their baskets of hair and all the poor ladies with their smaller baskets. They were all difficult to understand, like the people in the bearded man's book, *The Brothers Karamazov*. The title seemed to me like part of the litany of souls, a list of names long dead, crackling on my tongue as I pronounced it. I could not understand the book, and I skipped pages, but I plodded through it, because of Alyosha. I was in love with him and I thought he was I.

I wanted to be a monk, and I wanted him to kiss my hand, like he kissed Liza's. My grandmother was Father Zossima. Before she was taken out to be paraded, I took one last look at lipsticked, coiffured Father Zossima and wept and wept. She was going to stink in a short while, and I cried like a good monk. Many people pitied me, and the great Vice-Consul to Spain sat me in his lap. I sat still a while then struggled out of it, the smell of soap and fish, and went back to my post on the balcony, above the river. I tried to sit grave and quiet like Alyosha.

Soon the Abuelita left her house toward the church. The chief mourner broke plates outside the door. Candles were snuffed and from above I could see the waft of death. The flowers were taken out, the ribbons limp, the petals limper—they were dying, too, and looked so lonely. All the mahjong tables were emptied. The provincial governor, three municipal mayors, the Vice-Consul to Spain, and an old man whom no one knew but seemed to be the Abuelita's only other male relative carried the coffin by the handles carved out for them. The lawyer was sidelined as always, glancing cunningly, like a cur. I wanted to stick my tongue out at him, but I was Alyosha and kept still. The parade was about to start.

The Vice-Consul stood at the head of the town, black band on his arm like the rest of the men; they all looked wounded. He kept waving a hand at my sister, but she wouldn't join him. She stood apart across the street, looking at the crowd. Someone pointed up, toward the river. Anna saw me. She came up the stairs then to the balcony, against the river. She was very beautiful in black, like Liza, and she took me by the hand. Amid the crisp smell of old ladies' powder, salt-mud smell of old men's grease, we were the only real people in the town, Liza and Alyosha. It was very hot, and down on the street people kept crowding around me, and my sister was beginning to speak to me in Spanish like my grandmother. I was stiff, holding the book in my hand. They didn't know I was Alyosha when they patted me on the head. They didn't know how much I was in love with them, I wished to be in love with the world I could see, trying to love the world like Alyosha. And I wept with Alyosha's bereavement, I sobbed with Alyosha's grief.

But to be honest, I was no Alyosha.

Even in death, I could not look at the Abuelita. I was not yet sure I had ever forgiven her, for my father's leaving, for confusing sorrows, old, distant hurts that were not even my own—because after all, the Abuelita had always loved me. And so I wailed before the people of Alang-Alang, in my guise as a bereaved child. Oh Alyosha.

B) Grade School Reading Curriculum. We read ghost stories, the poems of Henry Wadsworth Longfellow and Christina Rossetti, and Doctor Jose Rizal. Rizal kept butting into the curriculum from the time I was in Grade One. From grades one to six, I read about His Childhood, His Education, His Travels, His Novels, His Exile, and finally, why did it take so long, His Execution. I had to read about the poet's generosity, his love for his chickens, which he ate in the sinigang anyway, and his prodigious talents, which included fencing, sketching, watercolors, truth-telling, shadow puppetry, sculpture, letter-writing, ophthalmology, Europe-touring, propaganda-fomenting, lovemaking, foreign-language-speaking, abaca-planting, and cross-dressing. In high school, I had to read his novel *Noli Me Tangere* twice, once in English, in a corrupt version of sentimental miasma, and second in Tagalog, in a stark, lucid urgency that made me want to kill all Spaniards above ten years of age. In Spanish, I had to memorize his tragic poem, "Mi Último Adiós," written in prison and smuggled out in an oil lamp, like a scene in the *Count of Monte Cristo*, his favorite book when he was a child. I could tell he, too, was cursed with bibliolepsy, except he cursed the rest of us by also writing, not just reading. I grew up knowing Rizal's library—thus, also the legend of the Moth and the Flame, and the incredible Alpine story of William Tell. I was taught to be a reader through the stories about Rizal, and being so caught in his reflection, so held in his power, I tried very hard to escape.

It was a losing battle.

He kept wanting me to be nice, and to always love my country, no matter how stinky, and to raise high my brow serene, for reasons that I could not fathom. But I did not want to pity my country. I didn't even want to think about it. But my Grade School Reading Curriculum would not let me escape Doctor Jose Rizal.

There is, like the opium drip running in Kapitan Tiago's veins, the world of Rizal in me that I could not fend off. The Abuelita in her last days looked like the ravaged Doña Victorina, viuda de de Espadaña, in her abominable rouge and senile dementia. I began to see Rizal's Placido Penitentes all around me, and every sacristan looked tragic, carrying their limp, smoking censers, in their thin gowns and captive looks, their hair shining with too much brilliantine pomade. Mrs. Kierulf, the mad gray-eyed lady with scary hair who always came begging at our house for a bowl of rice at the height of noon, looked like Sisa, of course, but with a more basic backstory—drug addiction and a life as a runaway, in her case to Olongapo. And in truth, I have never wanted to be Maria Clara, that bride of piety and delusion who is the lynchpin of all of his work, but I could see, in my dim adolescence, why I needed her—a shred of devotion.

And I hate to say it, but I got caught in that Maria Clara clap-trap—I started going to church every day when the Abuelita died, as if church were my anchor in a perilous time, while Anna kept leaving me in Alang-Alang in the middle of the week to motor into Tacloban on a whim, or hitch a ride with a Swiss *Lonely Planet* traveler who was wandering a bit too far from William Tell's Alpine glories on a pump boat to Siquijor. Free of her burdens upon our grandmother's death, by that time she did not feel the need to have me along. But my stations of the cross ended when my sister suddenly appeared with the bell-bottomed poet she forgot to name, at first.

She said—Primi, pack your bags, we're heading to Manila.

Anna was aglow, her beauty like a church: still, perfect, smelling a bit mossy, but magisterial. Anna has the ability of suggesting absolute poise, even when she is in torn jeans and an ugly Peace-themed bandana. I had just come from church, where I had recited the whole morning the novena to Saint Anthony, the Wonder-Worker—*O wonderful St. Anthony, glorious on account of the fame of your miracles, and through the condescension of Jesus in coming in the form of a little child to rest in your arms, obtain for me of His bounty the grace which I ardently desire from the depths of my heart!* And I realized, when I saw Anna, on the doorstep of our home in Alang-Alang, how lonely I had been during all those days of saying novenas and being dumb and witless Maria Clara, and I rushed into her arms and howled.

Then I beat her up with my fists, for abandoning me.

But all she did was laugh.

C) The Bathroom Incident. I read her book of short stories everywhere, at the playground on the grassy basketball court, by the green seesaw with its peeling paint, in the kitchen while Marga, the Abuelita's loyal leftover maid, plucked a chicken, in the sala with its broken TV, in the bathroom that for no good reason had unfinished walls. Estrella Alfon was my companion in the months I had before leaving Alang-Alang. I was going to join Anna on her adventures. I clutched her slim book, a red thing studded with stars, like her name. I have had many loves, and this falling in with

Estrella Alfon had a kind of radiant body, like her words were on my skin, warming me in odd crevices, my clavicles, my bellybutton, that lightning streak that ran from my pubes to the inner thigh, and behind my knees. I had no idea why. Her stories were about provincial bourgeois observing the world with curious regard. But the thing is—every observer in Alfon was a woman. Her women had the calm passion of Anna, her disinterested affection. I touched my pubes to soothe the electric sensation. It was weird to be so aware of my body as I was reading a book. I was rereading my favorite story, "Low Wall," in the bathroom, and it occurred to me, as I read again about the girl's self-defense, her teenage valor in Manila's postwar slums, that I heard a rustling, too, in the bathroom's low wall, as if, like in the story, I'd see a boy's *mata de pelo*, his rough sun-brushed hair, peeking through a gap to stare at me. But I kept reading the book and I kept feeling my pubes because Estrella Alfon had that effect on me, as if she were telling me to be who I am, as I was, a girl with a body, an electric thrill in my hands as I read a book. And when I looked up and I saw his eyes, who knows if it was a cat or a kid, I smiled, gazing up at them, my fingers on my throbbing flesh, my own kind of freedom, sliding back and forth, back and forth, pressing my pleasure on my palm as I held up the book, Alfon, the star, toward those eyes.

D) College in Diliman. Two jeepney rides and a city away from my decrepit, proud Manila. I called Manila my own now, at sixteen disarmed by its frequent disasters, multiple futilities, abstraction of adolescent incompleteness. Although the "real" Manila—streets, schools, stones—impressed me like other places did: some santol seed flattened dry, actual taste unmemorable.

Trees in Diliman shield you noncommittally, acacia, narra, and caballero; there is no danger to hide from and no fear to face, but the trees guard broad and motherly. I went to history class and heard, with neither pleasure nor dislike, of things I'd long read about. I went to Spanish class and recovered the tedium in the Abuelita's speech, saw through the language my grandmother had spoken with such haughtiness the commonness of everybody's meanings, *la mesa, la cilla, la cosa.* I learned to see through another language the same sullen world. I had known people as the coming and leaving of people in boats, alien companions to whom one spoke in broad signs of ship politeness. Beginning school in Diliman, I knew no one and did not wish to.

Amid the monotone of my activity, the man who was my English teacher sometimes caught my attention. He usually found himself engaged, not in a debate with young, avidly distrustful minds, but in a hero's struggle with his stutter. He also reminded me of my brother-in-law, because he dressed so badly. By then, as I said, my sister had a husband, thirty-year-old Joaquin, who had such an unerringly awful sense of fashion I think it was his way of elevating himself to myth. My teacher dressed like Ray Conniff on his LPs. One afternoon, this man described a passage in a book he had read, and there was a quaver in his voice that sent the two girls beside me into soundless titters. The quaver seemed on the verge of cracking into his stutter, but his voice, swept up in his earnestness, steeled itself and sailed on.

My attention, idling on the gathering shadows of the trees outside, the snail-crawl glut of darkness, got caught on my teacher as I recognized the passage he was describing. The first pages. I recognized it with a thrill. The first glimpses into that warty woman's apartments, the pawnbroker's place, the city's riverine streets, the hero's fever. A book I had read on my own, for myself. My teacher had not mentioned the title of the book yet nor its author, but I knew, I knew what he was talking about, the scenes etched in my mind as if from my own past. I knew the feeling he was describing. Then he spoke of another. First pages—that was my teacher's theme. He was beginning to eat flowers and the crescent moon was in his eyes when he woke again. The woman running in the forest with the quasi-Japanese Quasimoto and the blue-eyed boy from Indiana. And before he said her name, I knew it: *Alma*: the words in the book an echo of memory, a waking dream. And when he spoke with reverence before the blank-faced class of the gift of the author's excited pen, the unfaltering gathering of the truths of emotion, I flushed as if I had written the books myself, I felt giddy with my elation, my skin thickened with my pride. And when he finally spoke the writers' names to the silent class, *Fyodor Dostoyevski, Wilfrido Nolledo*, it was as if glass had shattered, and the world had seen itself pure, and we were in the presence of a wondrous thing.

The name *Fyodor Dostoyevski*.

The name *Wilfrido Nolledo*, in stuttering guise.

It took me days to get over the idea that someone's attitude about a story might be equal to my own attachment—in the man's case, an aposiopetic enchantment. For several days, I walked the university with a different air, suspecting people of passion.

But very curiously, and I note this fact carefully, there was nothing remotely erotic that I could feel for that man. Maybe it was because, in his effort to keep from stuttering, his saliva sometimes spilled over and dripped delicately down the side of his face, like filthy rain. He was a mess.

16. Finally in Ermita

Anna had finally kicked off her shoes in Ermita, where she let herself rest after years of strange towns and eager men. She had met Joaquin in one of them, Sexmoan or Bolingan. I must have been on that trip when for some reason Anna's instinct for wandering and distraction clicked shut. It bothers me that I don't remember. But there it was, in her unequivocal way, Anna "fell in love," and I was lone official witness at the wedding. It was held in an office at the Manila City Hall. Paper documents of every citizen's birth, marriage, and hapless denouement graced her wedding aisle. Pulp dust like rice showers enveloped the bride. Anna wore a short dress in shiny synthetic cloth of a scarlet that threaded mistily into green. The design mapped a pale green about her breasts that slid into red about her belly, in the manner of a caimito, a ripening star apple.

When she bent slightly, peeking irreverently into the justice's ledger in the middle of the ceremony to anticipate her vows, her skirt, lifted by the bias in the waist, rose dangerously. Joaquin tugged it down. Anna slapped his hand off and peeked some more. The justice had stopped speaking.

Joaquin shouted: Anna!

Her dress was showing a full-length view of beach-thawed thighs and, as her skirt moved, intermittent, goosebumped borders of a sunless behind.

He tugged at her dress again.

My sister turned to her future husband.

I saw her glare in a familiar way, as when she had once said to my high school principal, "bugger off," in her best lush-like English manner, learned from the movies.

Again, Anna slapped his hand.

Joaquin slapped her face.

Anna bit him.

The justice was waving his arms, clerks were crowding around.

I held on to Anna, whose cheek was as red now as the scarlet of her dress, but it was unnecessary. Joaquin had his arm over both of us and was whispering a wordless rush. Anna was kissing him on the back of his neck, Joaquin was arching to reach her face, and I was thirteen, in the middle, wondering about my life.

PART TWO

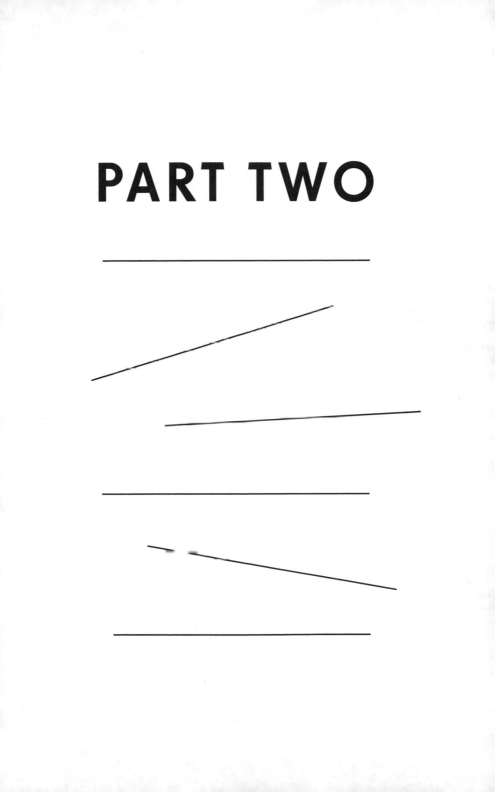

1. What compels me

What compels me to collect these memories, my *ficciones*, as if time were interested in itself, in the connections between minutes? When we all know how terribly difficult it is to get its attention, so engrossed is time in its feet or hands or whatever it is that occupies it so eternally? It seems one always writes in order to get its attention: hey look, this was you at 12:01 June 16: and this was you at 12:02 and so on, and you try to say 12:01 was related to 12:02, and all this led to 7:04, and see, you have meaning. But time is looking at its feet, unable to see beyond their actuality, an absorbed look on its face, mouth slightly puckered.

All stories seem to shout at you: minutes are blood relatives, they all connect like ordered cousins, and the beginning leads to the end, to some kind of philosophy, some furrowed forehead with a light bulb over its head. And I am not writing—and I say this above the fake-eyebrowed laughter of old women and the prim distaste of my not-so-cherubic coevals—to explain myself, mockery of Maria Clara. What impels me to this table, with its rather weak light, is not an idea about time or a need for meaning. What moves me is a grip on my throat, the inward glance at something passing, an impulse born of fast, unformed memory.

Iconic figures, still figures in sleep, gestures from the ragged mythology of my memory trap me; and in this moment's emptiness, I waylay them: I speak. I keep flapping words in the air like dirty blankets. I am careless with them when I know they are the only instruments I have toward the ordering of my knowledge of you—writing mainly on the impulse of love.

2. There must have been a key

And yet there must have been a key that wound up my subsequent "delirium," as a medical orderly once called it, yanking a system into motion. I flip over the folds and layers time dresses itself in and fumble across the bare hard back of the plastic doll, find the mechanical steel beneath the play-clothes, twist my hand and watch myself being hypnotized on a flowered orange and green couch in a condominium that showed Makati to me like an ordered Game of the Generals set, playing metals tipped over and revealing blank, silver bottoms.

The psychiatrist's trick didn't work on me. I didn't go into a trance.

But I obliged the doctor's anxious face by telling her the story of my brother-in-law who was sleeping in melon briefs in the room across mine, one morning when my sister was out and I was cutting my high school music class. And as I told her the tale, randomly picked in a dirty laundry of stories, it dawned upon me, miles above Makati's metallic sheen, that maybe here was a radix, the point of no return. The story grew into a tale of tendresse, and I felt a moistness between my thighs. And I remembered myself, fifteen years old, morose high school senior in a striped black and green shirt and morning mouth, pass by the "master's room" to get a glass of milk and the day's paper. I remembered the absurd sight of his melon briefs and his hand on the bulge in the center, while his legs were sprawled like a great baby's.

Joaquin used to wake late in the morning from writing late at night. For a time in the writer's circuit, especially after Anna had run away with a disc jockey for a jazz station during that third summer, he was a famously sullen iconoclastic poet who rendered in booze-voice his incomprehensible poems. I used to see him at those parties, a silent figure in the shadows or in the afterthought chairs around drinking tables, squeezed in as the seventh in tables for six. When I'd meet him, he'd always treat me in the grave way he had even in the house when I had been living with them those short three years. I remember in a haze getting him into one museum's bathroom, and all he did was pat me on the head, as if I were still fifteen.

He's been gone from this city for years. In a café, he once announced he was going to leave the stuff and bullshit altogether, and soon, but in the tradition of café evenings, no one minded him. That same evening he left Manila to live in the wilds of Cotabato, with what was reportedly a wilder young thing. Others report that he lives with no one. He's a hermit with a guitar whom barrio folk approach to notarize certain documents. His handwriting is clear and formal, they say, and his silence engages respect from all. Others say that he has attempted to form a rock band there, in a last-ditch pun on the place's name. No one has actually seen him. It seems the barrio's name keeps changing with every writer or friend who reports on him. Who knows if it turns out he is still just teaching at Santo Tomas, making his unreadable poems.

I went to him that morning, five years before this present date, in the shirt I have mentioned. Near him on his table were sheets of paper carefully arranged beside his typewriter, and at the head of the table was an ordered pile of books, and you might imagine me in mellow, unsentimental light and tilted, unflinching pose know his curls like wet wooden shavings and his body at first clammy like a corpse, and my own schoolgirl surprise at myself. I didn't bleed, and he had a belief in my looseness, I think, even when I was fifteen. I was, after all, Anna's sister, companion in all fruit seasons. Or maybe the weight of his midnight labors found him prepared for the strangeness of mornings, and I was another wave of poetic motion, entropic extension of nocturnal turnings of words, the last serendipitous rhyme.

Nothing much was made of it.

My sister—all unknowing, it seemed, with coincidence's lack of malice—packed our things once more some days afterward. She was moving into a season of jazz. She said I was old enough now, soon to go off to college. She gave me a bankbook with my share of the Abuelita's money, the proceeds from the Alang-Alang plaza and what was left of the barrios in Barugo, and the advanced rental receipt for an apartment on Adriatico where I was supposed to live. My sister thinks of everything. A few days before my birthday, I transferred all my belongings to Adriatico. Anna went to live on the haunches of Banahaw, where the jazz jockey was Second Clairvoyant in a sect for the length of time it took for my sister to leave him. I went back to Joaquin's house the day I turned sixteen, before I went off to college. It was empty, all the books gone, and the tables and chairs and Franz Kafka, almost as if water had swept through the place once more, stealthy as childhood.

Before the clumsy doctor who explained my life to me, I thought how paltry concepts of the id and various psychopathological superstructures might be beside my strange sudden delight at recollection. It might be true that I had substituted in Joaquin my dead father, and it was Joaquin doubling as Prospero whom I cherished guiltily beneath a Calibanic craze, but all abstractions wither into falseness, a dull ring, beside the emphatic skin of memory, this textural delight, extra-textual discovery. What had led me on my ghost-cruise around the lips and loins of words was basically this: the substance of recollection in my thighs, sharp response of flesh.

Not dead fathers in the vague unconscious but lives in the cunt, where pasts resurrect and spring surprises.

• • •

3. Somerset

In college in Diliman, I got to know Juan Somerset Chong. You've probably heard of him. He's published. He was a writer, and some people called him Jun or Johnny. I see him in my mind as W. Somerset Maugham, his white tokayo, Mister Short Story Master, magical organizer of time. He was prone to fat and booze, and his stories were always so conventional—forgivably so. He could pursue an objective correlative to its expected conclusion, like an ant finding its sugarplum or a wise pigeon going home. He was a natural at writing stories that I admired but could not stand.

He was my classmate in Greek and Roman Lit, a survey course. The class, an assortment of talkative virgins, studied schizophrenics, and macho men from La Salle who wore pink Lacoste shirts, moved in time from Homer to Aeschylus to pre-Vatican II Virgil. We ended on the usual alliterative question beloved of sophomores: Aeneas or Achilles? The class, of course, was on the side of Achilles. Why not? The guy was a stud. Our teacher, laywoman, we learned afterwards, in post-Vatican II Opus Dei, said Aeneas was the only satisfying hero in the history of world literature. Piety is all. The end. She won the debate, of course, ours being a semi-feudal, slightly futile system of education.

This isn't the point of my story, although it is interesting to note how, unconsciously on my part—I plead lack of cunning, I was going to experiment by writing this section completely off the top of my head, following the pseudo-Romanticism to which I still—in secret, of course—regress—if I may use that pejorative word—as I was saying, before this fear of realists and my fellow nerds overtook me, it was quite unconscious on my part that I started this second part of the story with some comment on semi-tragic figures, excess and hubris, as if it were foreshadowing, and I were a young little lambkin come back from the writing workshop in Silliman, stung and black and blue from the constant nudging at the elbow telling one to write the traditional, Aristotelian, New-Critical story, that's the only way to save your brooding soul. Write the traditional story, with beginning, middle, and end, with tangential divagations at strategic moments, and you're on your way to self-respect in Philippine Lit.

There are the six types of symbols, says Edith Tiempo, doyenne of the writing workshops. And the Maverick Symbol, she says, is the worst. Well, Ma'am Edith, though your world loves you and may you rest in piece, I wish to exhume The Maverick—that piece of the story puzzle that exists without a clue, neither here nor there, some wandering jew.

As for Homer, of course, I am your amateur—but I am once again getting ahead of my story. What can a bibliolept have against Homer? There's a scene with Hector, Achilles dragging Hector around like a comet with a magnificent tail: for Patroklos. How often I use such scenes to bolster me in my faith and fiction. I wish to snatch them from their contexts on the page and recreate them in me. I wish to believe Dante's Francesca da Rimini *is* me, Nastasia Philipovna *is* me, the mother in Estrella Alfon—Magnificence—*is* me. But they resist, they remain pristine in their texts, and inviolate. By no amount of either wishing or sophistry can one actually steal Francesca from Rimini (now a Fellini-esque carnival of a beach town in Italy anyway, with ceramic cetaceans and tourist bums—and not a castle of infernal love).

They live in their books.

And I lie in the shadows, preying on their passions, by which I authenticate myself like an antique without history, gathering dust in an obscure museum.

And as I grew older, my osmotic paranoia became more terrible. Often, I'd base ethical decisions upon how an author might behave. What would Dostoyevski do? It was a precarious investigation. Based on limited knowledge gained from imported journals and wordy prefaces,

E.g., Dostoyevski

1) took care of the orphaned children of his favorite brother Mikhail: thus, though a mad gambler he was a good uncle;

2) wrote his best novels in a flurry of poverty, in a matter of days, to stave off an evil publisher, Mephistopheles of the Russias, who was going to own the copyright to his next books if he didn't finish *Crime and Punishment* on time;

3) fell in love with his typist, like Borges, but unlike Joyce—

I would make daily decisions based on skimpy facts. I'd show excessive courtesy to people in the literary service industry, xerox operators and typists, for in a Philippine Saint Petersburg, they might help budding epileptic geniuses, lurking in places I'd missed. Once, I met this man, a typewriter repairman who fixed my manual Olympia, a gray space-alien-like affair. The university was a place, so distant and inconceivable now, swarming with typists and smelling of acrid mimeograph machines.

His shop was a bunch of cardboards and a wooden ledge and table. From the clothes and soap and scattered dishes on the floor, one could tell that he also slept in his shop, brushed his teeth amid the keys, et cetera. He was young, about my age, his hands were black from the ink of letters. He was brash, looked directly at my blouse, white and patterned with cross-stitched petals, bra strap looping through the fine embroidery, nipples crushed decorously against the white. He took my typewriter, its skull-like case and gaping abdomen, and tinkered with the metal, fingering the keys with the fond expertise of ancient craftsmen, who must always start off as child laborers. He was still a child. But as we discussed prices and damage, the revival of certain functions, tightening of screws, I couldn't help staring at his fingers, knobby, thick, and dirty, which knew all the mechanisms of these alphabets. Curves of S's, crotches in Z's, bulges in the B's.

I've always been amazed by specific, technical skills.

When I met him again, he told me the machine was fixed. I said I could not take it to my dorm; it was too heavy. After he deposited it by the dorm desk, I asked him questions, Dostoyevski-like. We walked to the Sunken Garden and all, that wide lovely emptiness. With this boy, the ground seemed more straightforward, and in fact I remember its grittiness and the discomfort of insects and the typewriter repairman's weird gesture. He would not open his eyes, and blindly, from beneath me, he took a nipple without hesitation, exactly as if it were a standard Q on the extreme left side of a board, and squeezed with a scratching fingernail motion, a man who was good at his job. And I understood Dostoyevski, who may have fallen in love merely at the sight of a hand moving skillfully upon bland keys.

JUAN SOMERSET CHONG wrote action stories, linear, hard-punching stories about over-achieving nihilists. His heroes were always male, over thirty, and destined for self-destruction. They were NBI spies, NPA malcontents, or rich, lonely loonies who became communists to fulfill themselves. There was a rabid morbidity in his stories that critics disliked (and still dislike) because they believed his bulldozing belief in the triumph of evil was, in its own way, a perversion of the world's natural dialectical motion. In actual life, Somerset was a staunch national democrat before the first EDSA rebellion, a critical delineator of leftist atomist policies after it, a meticulously faithful husband, and a conscientious student who used sarcasm in his papers only as a last resort. After Joaquin, he was the first published writer I met, although his work written before martial law had been banned because most of his characters at the time, those dead-end men, compulsively quoted Mao Tse Tung. Now that they quoted Lévi-Strauss and Gramsci, his characters were in print, though still unread.

I enjoyed Somerset's stories when I found a pile of them in the Palanca Junkshop, a vast, rat-infested room even poverty-line scavengers have overlooked, frequented by English majors when they want their papers to be perverse, a badly lit storeroom soggy with the rainsick smell of unread work. In spite of oneself, one feels a weakness breaking on the skin, a slight-fevered illness, at the mere smell of the room: cockroached *claritas*, fortress of failure. Seated on a stool amid the mess, the waiting snakes and salamanders (even the guard had refused to go in, and I had to switch lights on myself, wade through folders and fasteners heaped like dead cats in heaven, walk carefully lest I step on a ninth life, one writer's last shot at death), I read his work. Moments in Somerset's stories would surprise me, his language escaping simple-minded theory guilelessly to make me happy.

Somerset was older than everyone in the class because he had quit school ten years before to become agitator at anti-imperialism rallies. Being a reasonable man, he quit that, too, when he married and got rich quick selling used Japanese clothes—which he got extra-cheap from a boyhood friend, a smuggler who rules the South China Sea and is also one of his recurring minor characters. At his leisure at thirty years old, he was back at school, large-bellied like a legend, which he was, for the thirteen consecutive Palanca Memorial Literature Contests he had joined and failed to win, much to no social realist's surprise. He's a curious artifact, a rational bibliolept with ordered sanity. I see him among the World of Forms, or as the still buddhic notion of perfected author-ether; an efficient time-keeper as well, nailing a tale's errant syntax to some illusion of order.

We would have conversations about: the length of time it took him to write a story, how he got ideas, whether he woke up in the night thinking of a character, the superstitions he engaged in once the Palanca Memorial Literature Contests were about to be announced (he induced dreams of snakes, because snake dreams in the Chinese tradition meant good luck: he read encyclopedia articles about them, perused snake books at National Bookstore, visited the tanks at Manila Zoo; in all the time he'd been writing for the Palancas, he never dreamed of snakes—instead, in one dream in August a molar fell out of his mouth. Upon waking from the dream, he knocked on the headboard of his bed, waking up his wife, to whom he could not explain his anxiety because to tell about the bad-luck tooth would bring the impending disaster upon her. He kept it to himself until September, when the Palancas were announced and, as usual, he didn't win).

There's a June to September insanity that runs through writers every year, the season of the Palancas. The deadline for the only writing prize in the country that has outlasted dictators, earthquakes, lava flows, value-added taxes, and fierce internecine warfare among soft drinks bottling companies is some date in June. In September the prizes are announced, and in between sane women walk in a morass of anxiety alternating with thrill: the bug-eyed look of triumph when the name is called at the ceremony, and the writer gets her just reward, after the nights of toil and kowtowing to bad editors of daily rags, who tell her: I want some interviews, please, no personal essays: while her editor goes on to write his encomiums to Korean airline companies and supplements on Meralco, Manila's electric company that has no need of advertising, being a monopoly.

The Palanca is her just reward, after days of grueling work on semi-colons only to see them appear without bottom or carelessly undone, for there is not much for the Filipino writer but the Palancas. Even when you're published, the indifference of the experts will kill you.

AT ONE POINT, in this season of the Palancas, it seems that the logical end of bibliolepsy is the need to write. One begins to feel that one sits by the minus sign as reader. You are a nonentity, waiting only for words to devour you. On the other side is the positive sign, the Actor, the writer—the one who fulfills and is whole.

While talking with Somerset, something unfortunate happened. I wished a transposition to occur in the equation. I wished to write.

It was ambition by osmosis. Surrounded by language-passion, one couldn't help but get tainted. Inch by inch the wish seeped into what was once fresh water, one's innocent reading life, until you felt sticky with salt, soaked in an unavoidable estuarial stench, submerged duckling, doomed Bird-of-Speech.

These thoughts are the scourge of adolescents, ambition of

the idle. There's a scorn in you, a weakness, a tenderness, a fury. A derision for the world, an ache for it. There's a fire in you, and all the world is fuel. And soon, any object, all persons, become prey to your tenderness. It's a maddening thing.

In my case, voices got in the way. In me were the chimes of different moods and tenses, three-pronged persons and declining cases, plurals of attitudes, stresses of divergent time, prosodic differentiations apportioned by memory. And all the other books I had ever read. Not to mention rampant feelings of ineptitude, dismay in lucid moments as one regards one's ignorance—of the physical laws that hold narrative tension together, suspensions, wires and cables and the precise intuitive calculations of what fits or does not.

In a mood of lightness, one might reach for the past tense, telling a story with few digressions. The indicative past seems a public mood, a day mood that only watches. But another voice crowds: this present tense, swaying in a dew-ish innocence, in a kind of meta-time. The present tense holds reserves of a lost-and-found gush of love, splashing in one like stoned water, spurting forth at intervals from a reservoir of abstract longing. It spills spontaneously as if the reservoir were always too full—and the spill and the splash are released in this mood, out of time with the story.

Through it all, wild anxiety tumbles about, madly deleting then squinting at words, sorry and suicidal and much aggrieved by its thankless task.

I locked myself in my room, fed on leftovers from a biscuit tin. The next day, I forgot to go to school. In three days, my skin grew scaly from bathlessness and humid from sweat. Sores grew on my tongue and mold around the room. Rats' feet pecked on the eaves like rain, cat-cries in the night rain died like infants. Rainwind sang like bad blood in the night, blood sparked in my fingers like wet fuse.

All of the above were the deadly cadences of the story.

But words fell flat.

A bibliolept is burdened by all stories she reads, by other people's poems in her head. Dead people's words are in her like blood and bile.

Writing is not her vocation. Writing is an irrational detour.

The world needs more readers, not writers.

I cut my hair in a mirror. I gathered my incompetent curls and dragged the scissors three times through them. Snip through the sides, snap down the bangs. They fell to the floor. My hair sprawled still, as if waiting for my face again, surprised to find itself horizontal. In the mirror, my face was small, like a child's.

I felt better, shorn of my delusion.

I rode the first jeep out the next morning and found myself on Recto. The smell of Quiapo was stale, even in the early morning. I saw the stalls of second-hand books lining Recto and the Avenida, a straggling column of weak houses. Abandoned writers were in them, discarded imagined lives. I stood before one, looking at the titles, the books precariously on their sides, showing their spines, like rumps. Here they lay in this rat-nose place. T. S. Eliot is covered in molding plastic. Here is Djuna Barnes, unreasonably inert and further murdered by the Avenida air. Here's her neighbor, e.e. cummings, who used to yell at her on Patchin Place: "Are ya still alive, Djuna?!" In Manila, both of them were very dead. Finally, look at the omnipresent Rizal. His books were tumbled around the stall in various aspects of carelessness. While I was growing up, his language had acted as some daemon in my country's history, lurking in places and times like the inexhaustible scent of Banahaw ferns. And here he was now, being kicked around like squashed seed. I saw journals, old dictionaries, medical textbooks, rotting spellers. All discarded books cry out to a bibliolept an unmistakable alarm.

Save us, save us.

A stiff wind seemed to attempt movement above the street. It was only the exhaust from jeeps that roofed my city in movable etchings, charcoal and ink. I've always viewed this city as having been blue and green once, a pastoral glimpse I wish upon the asphalt. But here were the bad jeeps and old mudwater.

Avenida Rizal restored to me the city's faithlessness and filth.

I turned my attention to the books. I decided, before these books, this was where my passion lay. Bibliolepsy had misled me to become a writer. But I was moved by the world only because I was a reader. Writing was a mistaken corollary of my illness, an illogical branch of a simple syllogism. This was my logical conclusion:

I read, therefore I am.

That was enough for one human being.

My city loosened about me. Something went slack. The exertion of writing had screwed my skin tight. My skin moved into original rest. I unwound and breathed and felt lost.

Given this occurrence, what was left for me to do? I bought all the books mentioned in this chapter and even some titles from preceding ones. I was stuffing them into my bag when the barker of my next adventure came ambling towards me, with similar intentions, glancing at the books with the lean look of hunting men, although his face was fat.

I met up with Somerset at the bookstalls on the Avenida, and he invited me to my first poetry reading.

4. A writer's desserts

Poetry Reading: activity on the fringe of the city's nightlife, occurring beneath the smell of esteros and lechon manok, beyond the whirligig motions of open jeeps and locked-up buses and into the trim lawns of literate foreigners or the sprawling space of Jesuit schools or the maze of museums and art galleries where plaster busts are etched on the moss of brick walls, exposed to drunks in the open air.

Book Launching: a book may be launched many times; by the publisher, by the academe to which the author sullenly owes his bread, by the author's relatives or favored sponsor, i.e., British Council dilettante, favorite godmother, or suitor-pest from Budapest. Sometimes, the sponsor of the launching may be all three in one: publisher, academic dean, and mother. If any visitor to the Philippine literary scene is puzzled by the number of book launchings, he need only address this sorry fact: no one in a country of seventy million reads much Filipino Lit, not even their collegial writers, and the book launching is often all the sad author has for her pains, if she doesn't win—

The Palancas or magazine awards: the lumpen author's one shot at a lump sum.

5. First poetry reading

We got there in Somerset's car.

"Nice haircut," Somerset said.

"Thanks," I mumbled.

I looked at my face in the front-seat mirror. I looked like a celibate meditating on its bones. My nape was naked. Strands of hair flew from my face. I took out from my bag an old hat. I put it over my hideous scalp.

It was a straw hat I got from a Sagada summer, chosen by Anna the way she used to pick my clothes and shoes. Her husband the poet, or maybe it was another lover, the disc jockey, had recited a poem by a stream.

By what lever do certain poems revert to your hands, unbidden like coins from a machine? *I am born in your light I shipwreck.*

Salvatore Quasimodo. A forgotten poet. No one ever thinks about him. I found one of his books, *Selected Poems*, in translation, with the Italian all on the left, and wrapped lovingly by someone in plastic, at Avenida Rizal.

Salvatore Quasimodo, Salvatore Quasimodo.

I repeated a poet's name in my head, as if he might protect me from enchantment.

Somerset moved into a laze of Greenhills streets and slowed before a neat mansion. Outside the house, a pair of anthropoidal plasters, larger than life, faced each other. By the door, I looked at the absence of chairs from the sala, the dull surrealism of paintings on the wall. Faces of readers settle easily into disdain or what seems a proud boredom, which then becomes a fishlike blankness: in my view, the expression is only a function of a capacity for happiness.

Predictable people go to these parties. English majors and struggling painters, actors and jealous wives, activists and jazz singers and jobless millionaires. Who was I introduced to? Two drunk poets of interchangeable hue, one's face graven like a field anito, the other effaced like a mystic turtle. The slackness of the turtle's face was dramatic, chin gone, face so flaccid he looked as if he didn't have the muscles to do diphthongs. There was a spiritista trying to levitate between bilingual spells, and a group of surly young dramatists practicing their ennui before a bust of

Brecht. One man returned to a table to roll joints, in incremental repetition like the room's active rhyme. By the john, I was met by a groupie and her fictionist trying out methods of exposition in the dark.

At the door leading to the garden, a publisher tried his stature on for size. The turtle ran out of the house to vomit on the grass. Soon the garden's center was cleared for the poets' reading. Who was to save me from my scorn? I walked farther down the garden. Beyond my vision the turtle-faced poet was reading his poem. It was about the ears of Baudelaire or somebody's neuralgia. He managed to speak without slurring. I walked beyond the poets and into the shade of an exhaustion. I half-leaned on the trunk of a coconut tree, felt its low branches limply fan me. It was a failed bonsai, tall as your average poet. The lightness of its leaves brushed my hat off my head. My chopped hair drooped like shipwrecked weed.

Poets who finished reading regressed to this part of the dark. The turtle-faced poet came upon me.

"Well?" he said, his finger circling nervously round his beer, his chinlessness shining in the moonlight. "I wrote it when it was dark, you know, a darkness that made me deaf. I mean, all my senses go, but what I really feel is the loss of sound. The whole of Manila was dark and the moon wasn't out. Pain! I wonder if anyone has ever felt it? The total failure of the senses, because of a simple blackout! And I felt, this is living! When the body has deserted you, and space folds up, and still a poem is in your hand demanding light! more light!—"

"It was just a brownout, silly. Meralco needs to get its act together. It's a political failure, not a poetic incident."

The bilingual levitator was a news analyst and literary critic.

Men like these thwart my calling. Here is a piece of shoddy pride, the poet begging for your homage, one eye cocked to the moon, as if in secret only heaven might understand his poem while it is earth that must pay dues. I'm made for adoring, I'm made to be held in incoherent empathy with their stammering passion. But does he have to sound so stupid?

Don't think that I'm complaining, that I'm losing the thread of a reader's tenderness. Don't think this brief protest is a sign of weakening of my affection. Many have maligned my kind—I think particularly of memorious malodorous Lyuba, the indefatigable reader in a forgettable book by an otherwise great writer, pp. 81–84, McGraw Hill, New York, 1971. I think of Updike's lonely college teachers stalking Bech in the books. I think of Salinger's general unaccountable dislike of my species, Lector Amorosa, *sin duda sin pesar*. I think of Professor Lionel Lector himself, sine verbis, non esse, whose silence, so legend says, reprimands his readers, and yet we will follow him to his wordless grave.

A sexist layer of writer's crock overlays such portrayals of bibliolepts. Nabokov was no independent savant. He existed on the kindness of Vera's adoration, her waspish wit. And John Updike will one day be irrelevant, for all his elegant prose that still stabs me in the back, my body prickling at his precision. He has this vague aroma, an offal of chivalry that stinks of the chauvinist, that I, his adoring reader, will not shake off. And Salinger—well, he's a shell-shocked man. If it weren't for Esmé, her love, not his squalor, where would his gaunt art be?

This clinging avidity, this cloying reader's love that many writers scorn in public, *this* is my virtue.

O Cynara, I have loved you in my fashion.

So—sorry, my disgust before this turtle is aberrant, unmeant.

But I beg no pardon for the fact that he is excluded from the rest of my story, relegated to mere illustrative detail, like my hat.

It is a dark, stunted man who is this block of action's tardy poet.

Somerset had wandered off to his own sphere of levitation. The rule of a poetry reading is: every reader to her own wolf. His name was Domingo Cantero, a simple, lewd man whose hands, amazingly gentle and amazingly huge, cupped my breast's spider like a bloody web beneath my shirt, basic line of offence. It was a careless donation, indifferent as an autograph. But the thoroughness of his signature was pleasant, an enveloping gift. We first retreated to a nook in the den between the john and a shelf of books. Several turns and then, at his studio on this mat, stench for furniture, books for tawdry props.

From start to finish, Domingo's hands were moist and clammy as if the moistness sought permission for deeper perversion.

This episode sprung from bitter beer, with that sediment at the bottom of efficiently recycled San Miguel bottles: I had left my post by the tree and returned to the arena of the text's pale

shadows, these authors of my discontent. There was comfort in
the wick-wan liquid that trotted keenly down the spine. The ruin
of many authors has been from the high hooves of this traveling
warmth. No one says much about the drunkenness of readers.

At first I couldn't be bothered by the pain Domingo held mys-
teriously in his hand when we fled to his studio. Before I felt
the blood and bruises on my thighs and arms, I was already wet
and putrid from the path of his first palm. Later I saw it was a
simple object. A metal bookmark. I scraped it about him—I made
scratches all across his chest. The tip of it was the shape of a rabbit's
ears. On the commemorative handle were the words: Thornton
W. Burgess, Massachusetts. It had an inner metal that formed a
clip to hug a book's page. On this there was blood. Digging into
our flesh, this object alternately slashed and caressed me coldly,
and then I bloodied his wrists, holding it tightly in my palm.

In the morning when he looked at me, this poet of the first
reading cried.

He asked me my name.

I had read Domingo Cantero's poetry before, in one of those
journals that never go through a second volume. His work is lucid
and spare, descended from no tradition in Philippine literature.
He chooses to be sullen without rancor, to be amorous without
faith. To most readers, he is uninspiring and cold, and these
readers are correct. The starkness of his poetry belies, of course,
the baroque turpitude of his hands. I once imagined beneath the
skeletal calm of his work the ineptitude of an expansive heart.

I felt strange looking at his nocturnal face that mocked the morning's clarity. Domingo Cantero was not pretty. His forehead was broadly apelike, and between sobs his mouth disclosed perfectly set, perfectly incongruous teeth. His hands were as large as I remembered them, flourlike, wildly wrinkled in the palm, like a gentle chimpanzee's. He could have been some other chordate, a monkey, horse, or a hyena, but his whimpering was distinctly human: febrile, insipid.

Why should anyone weep?

He was sorry for the bruises and blood. I could not tell if it was for his body or my own. I could only watch his display, his enactment before me of the pain I was supposed to feel, and soon I became impatient and soon left the mat. And even though my back hurt as if I had bent over a dozen bowling balls, and my thighs seemed simultaneously swollen and hard like the mumps and disintegrate and shaken like jelly, while bruises awakened as I stood up, I bathed calmly.

Eventually, Domingo made me coffee. Through bath and breakfast he carried on like a clumsy epilogue, one of those that explain in exact and excessive detail the life of a character in which one has already lost interest. His sleepwalking as a child, the near murder of his mother (when he had stolen the family car and almost run her over by accident), how it had happened like this only once before, in Sweden, with a bottle of Aquavit and a small bottle opener or some equally strange tale, but that time with a blond fellow poet from Arhus. I had bruises mainly, few wounds, put clothes on without difficulty, and accepted his lame, voluble help.

Why should anyone weep?

I remember now the hand's giant movement on my body, epiphany of parts, molding of contour. And my own excavations—the tracking of his silent veins. Lastly, sculpting and chiseling, formal matters: these were above and beyond the incompetence of post-textual affections—pity and fear.

Like a reader past catharsis, I absolved pain by evoking the value of narrative remembrance, summoning the exclusive tenderness of texts.

People may get beaten up in books, may gouge their eyes out. When the reader doesn't cry, is it because she is unmoved? I believe in a grace much deeper than vulgar empathy, tenuous as redemption. When a reading is over, the revelation of plot's shape in the end and the unworded memory of text or body—the phrase made flesh that lingers, the stray savor in the tongue—these subvert the cheap response to climactic grief, restore us.

6. Second poetry reading

Somerset was genuinely remorseful the next day.

"Where were you? I looked for you all over. They said you went home with some drunk."

I shrugged. Dressed in jeans and clean all over, I was snug again in my apartment in the Ermita district, answering phones.

I was seventeen, and I felt my life was coming together, gathering into some purpose: I knew what I wanted.

"Where's the next reading," I asked. "And who was the guy by the piano, hovering over my old brother-in-law?"

I had mentioned that early in the evening, amid the turtles, psychics, and sundry psychedelics, I had stumbled upon a groupie and her writer by the john. The couple turned out to include my brother-in-law Joaquin. He'd been partly unrecognizable—although I should have known it was him, by his bright-green floral pants, widely flared at the cuffs. Joaquin's face settled into the politeness I knew well. He asked me how I was. His hand still threatened a dark shoot beneath the woman's shirt, sharp and ripe and glaring, her young, wide eyes daring me to question her rightness in his arms.

Fine, I said, and I was almost done with school. And Anna was still carving gods out of Banahaw stone, her face all red and happy the last time I saw her, from mountain heat and free profanity: you know Anna.

A nod was all I got. He was busy.

Hovering about Joaquin was this pale atrophied guy, playing the piano with the lid closed. He seemed to know Joaquin, nodding at him while we talked, and seemed to be waiting until we finished speaking. In the meantime he was playing some sonata on blank wood, eyeglasses bobbing as he swayed.

When I turned to pass him he looked straight at me, frontally, in a terrifying, crazed way.

"Who was that?" I asked Somerset on the phone.

"You're interested in a lunatic air-pianist? What's your problem, Primi?"

That was the first of many such questions Somerset asked.

But Somerset invited me anyway to the next event, at a sausage eatery on EDSA.

His name was Vincent Sabado, and the coincidence of this nomenclature, Domingo to Sabado, led me to a sense of my mission: my plot was on the right track.

Sabado was a member of a corporation of poets that called themselves c.l.a.p. Perhaps the acronym was a pun on the illness of nineteenth-century poets. Perhaps it meant something significant. Sabado was only an associate, a lowly organelle in a petri dish of superior nuclei. His group had struck a blow against the indifference of the Filipino audience by banding together, much like the Justice League of America. Ten poets are greater than one. And maybe, like Flash Gordon, Aquaman, and Green Lantern, each poet ruled over his own sphere of influence, epic, lyric, or diuretic, holding sway over different elements of nature—land, air, and sea. I imagine that these bondings, covalent or otherwise, must occur often among this country's writers who swim in a self-contained current in which they keep meeting only each other and are often each other's only readers, if they are lucky.

Writing may be a form of solitude, but it need not be a kind of punishment. In this country, writers are incarcerated not by political beliefs but by indifference. When books are said to have been banned in this country it puzzles me. After all, our writers are already exiles, closeted in their enclaves among those who know them, their fellow writers. Why ban those to whom so few pay scant attention and so many none at all?

In this case, for instance, Vincent Sabado was unknown to me until I saw him play a ghost piano in a dark room.

Meeting him had been a matter of chance. Snaring him required vocation.

I first went off to read his books.

I visited National Bookstore, Bookmark, Goodwill. None of them had his work. So I went off to Avenida Rizal.

The Avenida was engrossed in its usual mob of people, like a grave Go player hoarding pieces here, loosening up there. Students rushed with linear force down the street, notebooks held in a light, faithful grip. Workmen grouped before a movie poster (breasts for breakfast, cunt for lunch) while a morbid beggar sucked his lip, rattling his loyal money can. There by the theater with the giant posters of starlet meat, beggars brought the ravishment of flesh down to size.

Hawkers of endless trivia ranged their goods—cat posters, crucifixes, comic books with colored rape scenes, cacti, and calendars; one sold, inexplicably, black and white pictures of a bare right hand, palm clear and unlined. They looked strangely like Domingo Cantero's, and I turned a picture around not to see it.

A fruit seller was selling one of Anna's favorites, green tamarinds. Anna and I were scheduled to meet that week. I bought a
bagful for her, though I stood there imagining the lead content
in the snug, green tamarind flesh. The canals, filled with black
August rain, schemed silently. I smelled the stench of old women
without underpants, peeing in their skirts. This Manila smell
was the smell, too, of something from my childhood: I sniffed
to remember—the old school building, I thought: the belfry-like
grounds of Alang-Alang Municipal Elementary School Library.
Old women used to stand outside after mass at the church down
the street. Delicately, by the library wall, they would lift their
Sunday hems and liberate harmlessly their slow sediment of
grace.

The dark smell of fruit—still mangoes, joyless naranjitas—was
no match against the canal's stagnant wealth. And I, amid this
elaborate mess, was happy. The night with Domingo retreated,
a casual sadness aroused occasionally, alarmingly, by the brush
of cloth against bruised lengths of my skin. I walked carefully.
I picked my way through crowds, dawdled before a pile of penknives, hummed. A man walked by me, umbrella in one hand,
book in another. He wore a ghostlike goatee, hair thin but pre-
cisely cut. I watched him go through each stall, pedantically lifting
a dictionary, then a volume of de Sade. He seemed to lick the
crevices of a hardbound book in French. But in fact he was merely
myopically noting its firm, threaded binding, and approving its
fine quality. I liked his show of seriousness. It made me happy.

I found Sabado's book, not in an outdoor shack but in a bookstore with actual walls and a Chinese shopkeeper. There weren't many books in it, but the place was small, and it seemed as if the store were overflowing. The minute I walked in, the strum of a guitar met me. I tried to make out how the man arranged the books in the place. His technique was not alphabetical, topical, or geographic.

"Pedant," he said when I mentioned Sabado's name. The man had the inner-skin color of a straightforwardly murdered cat, ready for disgorgement of entrails and impending display in a dusty room. He was gray and deceptive of weight: he looked blubbery and lank at the same time. He had nappy blotches about his arms and back, a map of moles displayed by his limp-billowed sando. I perceived then that that was how he shelved his books. By his opinion of them.

He spoke in English. I learned later that he had been a professor in Peking when it had still been spelled that way.

He led me down an aisle—a short shelf that contained different editions of Joyce with a slim book of Li Po in their midst.

"Random sensualists," he pointed at them accusingly, when he saw what I was looking at.

On another shelf, sets of Murasaki were beside Proust, along with some gardening manuals. He parted the shell curtain that opened to a dim room. It was full of dust-filled boxes. I started to sneeze. Without turning on the light, he rummaged through a box and soon gave me Sabado's two books.

As a poet, Sabado had the stern style of one who wrote in a single, ideological mode. He believed the quatrain was a superior art, and the iambic tetrameter was its sole measure. Thus, his poetry sounded like a man with his prick in a door: squeezed and shuttered. The strangeness of his stance lay in the fact that he was only twenty-four. At so young an age, he had never experimented with free verse. It was diabolical. His other book contained his essays on Filipino poets who'd been born in the 1890s, a mixed brood of talent, and their subsequent post-cursors in English. He tried to fit the history of Filipino literature in English, *Volume I, 1899-1944, From the Revolution to MacArthur*, into a slim volume of slick material. He was good at gossip, the movie extra-hood of a poet in Stockton, California, the tragic cannery life of poets in Alaska. As expected, *Volume II, 1945 to the present, From Independence to Dictatorship*, was non-existent, a black hole of book launchings beyond even Sabado's prodigious abilities to exhume. I supposed his obsessions marked him as a possible loony. But some forms of insanity are more charming than others.

LET'S NOT GO into a rehash of the ghoulash and tripe of the evening—recycling of an event easy enough to imagine, although it does seem startling to recite poetry amid dangling Polish meat. Poets must go where sponsors take them, and the readers with them, duly shaking the aptly porcine bones of the Austrian-German importer of hams and happily imbibing his local beer.

As Somerset promised, Sabado was there, and I was introduced.

The fact is, most men, when faced with young strange women with an agenda on their hands, are shy. A girl must listen to her counsel, and it is as basic as a movie reviewer's manual. Will she disarm him by forthrightness or steal him by scorn? Or one may mix one's wiles, the way one does paint. Dab strongly here, dilute there, follow up quickly on a fresh assault, or let go until the canvas wants, once again, your brush.

A man, too, may take his stance. Attack, ignore, or candidly captivate. A girl may, of course, merely wait, mimicking useless statuary, like a charlatan's empty-eyed Muse.

Again, Sabado gave me that red-eyed glare he'd shown above the piano:

"Foreigner?" he barked out.

For a poet, his method was not unusual. He was rude.

"No," I said.

"You're lying. You have un-Filipino blood."

"You're right. Chinese on my father's side."

"And American," he accused.

I was self-conscious about my abnormal pallor, the bane of my childhood. In self-defense I stared him down.

He had wispy, curly hair receding at the forehead—a bad sign in one still young. This made his face look longer than nature intended it—his entire geometry was mainly vertical, in fact. His body, like his face, was as skinny as a book of poems. But his long back was bent a bit from a habit of shyness, like a book's water-damaged spine.

I was satisfied by his clothing. It looked like his poetry—a long-sleeved, collared white shirt, tightly buttoned at the top. The formality of it contrasted somewhat with his uncombed curls. He looked as if, unwashed, he were going to his first communion.

"Yes," I said, "Spanish and American on my mother's side."

He nodded, satisfied like a sleuth.

"Here, a drink," he said, glaring.

"I know your poems," I said, taking a reader's direct attack.

"You don't know enough," he spat, then said, bulging eyes directly upon me: "Whether I dwell within the heart of you/ I must know./ Tomorrow when the daylight lights the sky,/ Words must fly."

I started laughing.

"That's Marcelo de Gracia Concepcion. It's corny, and it isn't yours."

"You're right. I can get worse. Faigao," he corrected. "Cornelio Festin Faigao. Not Marcelo de Gracia. But that was a good guess." He was impressed. My research had worked. "Yeah, it's a corny poem. But rather likeable, don't you think? Like a heavy kind of old-fashioned toy. That's why I study them, those born before the war." He smiled widely at me: and he looked again like that crazed man in the darkness that I had first seen by the piano—large teeth and watery eyes glittering, possessed by some impediment to sanity.

I was charmed, smiling back.

He was standing as if slumped against the pork counter. Unusually tall, for a poet. He'd relaxed.

THE EASE OF a man's surrender surprises no one. As they say, he's lost a rib. Males have a hollow space that seeks completion. They are people with gaping holes inside of them, sad, incomplete anatomies.

My sister Anna told me that.

In a reader: what hollowness is filled? I once heard the first lines of a poem out loud. My introduction to the poem was in a sleepy classroom, fan dustily whirring—and what was sprung in me? The chain of response is clitoral, quick, like a spring in the loins, then gone. Just as we have Darwinian gills, our nerves seem to contain fossil lives. We are ready to spring at certain lines, as if a prehistory of reading slumbers within us.

Anna has said to me: Stop trying to justify your bad taste in men.

SABADO LIVED IN a high-rise in Malate. In his bedroom one saw the Bay, gangrenous with smoke but golden when one noticed. It was weeks before he took me there. I'd always meet him at parties, school, or fast food hangouts, where I held his hand like a dumb debutante, or we'd fumble furtively amid books in a stranger's house.

I thought he was not ill: only shy.

In his apartment lived his widowed father, erstwhile tricycle manufacturer, currently major dama player and enthusiast of all forms of curbside gambling—street chess, homemade poker, cardboard roulette, even games of holens, losing his marbles with truant kids in white polo uniforms who carried along their box-like, wheeled schoolbags without much shame. He frowned on the evils of organized jueteng and public-service lotteries. Like an agnostic refusing organized religion, he was proud of his simple lust for canto-boy jousts. Also living with Sabado were his two maids, a shallow aquarium of endangered rock turtles—when we were kids, my mother had refused to buy them, considering it a crime— and a cat named Simeon Villa.

Colonel Simeon Villa had been a doctor in Emilio Aguinaldo's revolutionary army and the author of "Aguinaldo's Odyssey," a diary of the flight of the Filipino heroes that ended in their tragic capture, by American troops and their evil dwarf accomplices, Pampanga's Macabebes, in Palanan in 1901. But Simeon Villa's claim to fame in Philippine lit is that he disowned his own child, Jose Garcia, for writing about sexual coconuts. Of course, we all know what happened. Jose Garcia Villa fled to his father's bitter enemy, America, to become the Pope of Greenwich Village and good friend of English, commas, and e.e. cummings.

Simeon Villa, the cat, had no poet progeny, Sabado said— just a handful of lice-filled beasts whom Sabado let out homeless on the streets the minute they could walk. One of his poems had been about murdering them in stoic plastic bags drowned casually in the Pasig, the piece written in sporadically iambic dismal couplets:

"Unmoored by tyranny of place,
They moved in tremor of grace."

Without beer, Sabado was a sentimental, even melodramatic man.

In his house, evidence of his father's presence was everywhere even when the old man was out: *Scientific American* by an armchair, shoe polish and large leather slip-ons by the door, and the ever-present aroma of brilliantine grease, a rich, florid smell. I'd spend time playing chess with this neurotic fading father, who liked to slap me, lightly but surely, on the hand when I'd play a knight:

"Another knight move?! Can't you see that flagrant check by the bishop of the king's open flank! It's clear as a snake in the Garden of Eden! Nitwit. Woman."

And he'd slap me on the wrist.

But I liked to play the knight, meandering in its intentions. It drove Sabado's mad father crazy.

He said I was a bad influence on his son.

Daily, on the dot, as light weighed heavily about Manila, Sabado's father would go down and spend his money on games in the street. Times like those, Sabado would bring me to his room. In the triteness of one's mind, a poet's habitat contains cigarette butts on the floor, Catullus about the pillows, sheets cleft by typewriters, and venerable puke stains on the rug.

Sabado's room was spotless. His books were Dewey-decimaled and arranged logo-side up, upright titled spines sweating in plastic. His white shirts, worn strictly twice, hung stiffly in his closets, which had varnished doors, hinges regularly oiled. He lived in a mad state of un-squalor, perpendicular to the vagrants on the street below. I liked the care with which he'd unzip his pants, the practiced declension of his disrobing. Shoes, socks, pants, glasses; buttons, sleeves, jesuitical briefs. And he'd take the position of hapless male, one with the unshod universe, chest heaving in a sweetly absurd manner, like a mutinous antique clock gone haywire. Like that silver dome upon the clock, his head's double glistens, reddening doppelganger, rotund like a Capitol, an amphitheater. Parliamentary procedure is oral. Labial legislation. On the dome and through the column, doric, corinthian, ionic, plate-tectonic, ice-cap tongue snorkeling a continent, fin-like berg having a blast. In the end, a still, sodden explosion shapes his flood, and the structure molts even as it shudders. Then I'm left with a soft carcass, a formless, Attic heap of rubble.

The first time one sucks a man to sap, there's inordinate pleasure in it. You think each movement is an invention, a kind of Magellan's land. And then of this sorry vegetable patch, you gain the intimacy of a scientist, an expert. What pride, what victory of knowledge! It is interesting to note how the tongue can turn into a species of joy—a flesh-to-flesh transubstantiation. At least for a moment in time.

And then he'd fall flat, limp, like a death.

My turn, I'd say.

I did enjoy this undertaking—but it was all Sabado requested of me. One-track, single-veined, he only wanted his.

He never gave.

Like a monk starving on specious principles, he had this notion of virginity, tacked onto his mind, I'd sometimes think, by a strange stern father who took his chess as seriously as he did the Vatican. At our separate moments of communion his father might as well have been guarding his son's chastity as ably as he won loose change on the street below.

Needless to say and nevertheless, or so he said, Sabado had never penetrated a vagina.

Honest to god. He swore. Upon Jose Garcia Villa, upon Angela Manalang Gloria. He couldn't do it—not before marriage. And he was determined to keep it that way, faith and fellatio intact, upon his honor.

To touch a vagina was like touching a chalice: a halo of God emanated from women, saying No Trespassing, not Hallelujah.

So instead he'd watch me.

My problem with masturbation is that it is anti-social. Having to concentrate so much on oneself, on expending the energy within you only to have it pop! into empty air—it defeats my purpose. I'm spent, but all I've given is small change. It stunts the possibilities of generosity.

On the positive side: there is the benefit of exploration. Knowing the matter between theory and praxis. For where is the vagina in all the books of romance and adventure? It's a hidden thing, secret as diabolical gold, and more neglected than Charles Bovary. At least of him, we know all the variegations of his childish hat, its tassels and lozenges and brim. But what has been essayed on the lapidary vagina? In a perfect time, in another universe, could some glorious Flaubertine have done for the clitoris what Flaubert did for the milliner's trade?

It is up to the woman to explore and know: the fact, for instance, that at first surface seems all—the graze of finger against central sliver. It seems almost that what operates thrill is not exactly touch, but the space between friction and finger, as of the light step of the skater over ice. And it will be well for one to study this tension carefully, like some medieval inquisitor or sleepless physicist, to note intently the minute gradations of space. One does this all on the radix, the bridge, for the rest hardly counts. Strangely, that great minotaur of mysteries, the secret within the forbidden—what's penetrable—is a bland, tense, but predictable bin. Readiness is in the fleshly line, exterior, and so is completion—what you must seek is the nib before the wall's breach, to which you cast a dorsal flick, terrible, and if it spoke it would keen.

• • •

I REMEMBER MYSELF and Sabado once in that dark, muffled interior, curtains drawn against Manila, engaged in this mutually exclusive inquisition; and there were the steps of his father on the stairs, the scratch of a knob. The air grew gross with suspense. Sabado swept my face from him, taking matters in hand, and jerked about in a desperate derangement. Love is curious and silly—for I used that word loosely then—I thought he looked so much like a fantastic icon of a writer, writhing about in a grim interiority, separate from all, with his flailing body and his mouth a petrified void, as he partook in a privacy no one could enter, and not even love could bear to look.

7. Third poetry reading

At this point in my story, I must pick and choose.

"You are headed for a Viernes Santo," Somerset said darkly.

We were in the school cafeteria.

"We're worried for you," he continued.

Bernard and Tina, our classmates, nodded their heads.

"There's steam rushing through you," Somerset warned: "you look as if you're moving to a boil."

Maybe it's writers, most of all, who do not understand a reader's compulsions. "*Hypocrite-lecteur*!" the poet had said. "*Mon semblable, mon frère!*" I believe the last part was merely charming assuagement from the poet, a significant afterthought, but an afterthought no less.

> *In this menagerie of mankind's vice,*
> *There's one supremely hideous and impure . . .*
> *I mean Ennui! who in his hookah dreams*
> *Produces hangmen and real tears together.*
> *How well you know this fastidious monster,*
> *reader—*
> *—Hypocrite reader, you—my double! my brother!*

We are blamed for many things—hammy paraphrases, indolent misperceptions, glibness with symbols and, of course, last but not least, the cheap pleasures of solipsism, boredom's gas   purloining lines for our own prurient testimonies, our vulgar quotidian lives. I myself resent those epigraphs in which an author takes an isolated quote to prop up his unrelated, shoddier work. Please take note of that. I read the poems Delmore Schwartz refused to publish in his lifetime, the poems in which he appropriated everyone, from Homer to endlessly resurrected Shakespeare, and I felt bad that the good taste he had upheld in his life by not publishing them had not reverted to his publishers when he died.

Hypocrite-reader, the writers say with bile; and with the grace of the cunning, they add: "My double! My brother!"

I am not fooled.

• • •

RIGHT NOW YOU think I am trying to elevate myself with this domino line of imprudent days. When in fact, you think, I am debased—I am diminished with each dropped name.

You bristle for your fellow-authors like TV housewives caught in the contests of detergent soaps: Reader, you say (even rhyming), you are only the shadow Brand X to his glistening, trademarked fame; you are the gray generic formula trailing behind his capitalized name. You will not be remembered, whereas the author—well, the author will at least be indexed or footnoted, even when he is reviled and/or incidentally put to shame.

Accepting humbly, then, my inconsequence and the implications of this tale, I will relate the story of Viernes Santo, picking and choosing judiciously from among a number of presentable candidates, semblables, freaks, frères, and others.

THE DOOR OF the cafeteria, which was housed in the Faculty Center, opened. It had a slow way of moving, this door—a bit like the careful, rheumatic movements of many of the people who frequented the place: old or aging professors with different measures of gall drained in them. The door opened but did not close. Instead, a head seemed to hold it ajar. It peeked through the door and looked into the room. Not looking, you'd say, but glaring, or almost as if startled into our presence—the flies on the food, the aluminum dullness of the counters, the grime on the cracked plywood walls, colored flesh now, withered to the hue of our questioning faces as we looked at him, he who seemed surprised by his own arrival.

His head, when seen this way, preening back as though ready to be sliced by the door, was all eyes—a wide gray reckoning of his place and time.

"Hey look," said Somerset. "It's Professor Lector."

He said this even though we all already knew who he was.

Professor Lionel Lector—though I don't recall my naïveté anything to be proud of was the reason I had decided to go to university at all, and this university in particular.

He was famous for one poem, a song of love and faith and dying, a common enough tale for any song, and a rare occurrence in being written so simply, powerfully, and completely, easy to memorize and quick to move the one who reads. It was a poem embedded in our national memory now, published as it is in grade school texts, definitive anthologies, commemorative books, and even periodically in the *Philippine Journal of Education* (as though it were a tic in this august body's neck). Even babies, it is said, were affected by this poem. They cried at the right parts. Or so Prospero had said to me. I would cry, turning my head into my sheets, when my father recited the penultimate line of grief.

"I thought he was dead," said burly but unsaintly Bernard.

"He should be," said Tina. "It's better than appearing mad like that. He gives me the creeps in the hallway, I think his dental fixtures will one day pop out. What's he always chewing on in his mouth—cotton balls?"

"When you are old and gray, Tina," I said, "I hope someone gives you a mirror and knocks it into your gums. I'd like to do that to you right now."

"Hey man," said Bernard, "chill out. It's cool, Prims: everybody knows we worship the Prof."

"He wrote only one poem after all," said Tina.

"That's not true," said Somerset.

"She's only joking, man," said Bernard, a placating kind of guy.

"Anyway, your joke's in bad taste," I answered, taking up my coffee cup without looking at them.

"Are you in love with him or something?" Tina said to me.

Bernard laughed.

I turned my chair and looked at the siopao and the bedraggled pancit steaming upon the counterpanes of our noontime slop.

When I turned back to the group, the Professor's head was gone. He wasn't in the room.

YOU KNOW ONE learns a lot from one event, sometimes from even the most innocuous ones. Spending a day talking frivolously with a group of friends, you feel upon walking away from the table a generous repulsion in your chest, like a cotton wad of gross but natural excretions. You feel that you've wasted time, it will not come back, and worse still, you wasted it posturing, peacocking your image, or cheaply frittering away your passion upon indifferent people—the usual feelings of self-loathing that come upon us in fitful times. And you think: Why do I even allow myself to speak?

It was like this that afternoon, as I walked out of the Faculty Center to my new apartment in Area Six. I had moved all my books to the university area. The trooping over from Adriatico to Diliman took a toll on my nerves. The daily diesel fumes were deadly. And as I passed by a room where people normally had classes, because of the shortage of space in the college, I saw again the old poet, Professor Lector, by a door.

His back looked like the upright back of an amphibian, leaning in.

"I like to look at them." He turned to me.

I was startled by his address.

His voice was loud; from the habit of years of teaching, which unduly modulates speech to this high treble.

He motioned me to move closer.

"Look at them," he was whispering. "It's my class."

"Then why aren't you teaching it, sir?" I asked.

"I am," he whispered, nodding his head. "They just don't know it."

"What are you teaching them, sir?" I asked.

"It's just this." He motioned me even closer to him, so that he said loudly in my ear: "It's that the author is dead. He is no longer in our midst."

And at that, he burst out laughing, so loud that the waiting students in the classroom turned all together to look at us and saw him practically keeling over from his mirth, a robust laughter that unmistakably swore he was alive.

THROUGH CIRCUMSTANCES AND an almost strange delicacy, I had never enrolled in his class. Professor Lector had never been my teacher, though I had decided to take the test for this school because I knew he taught there. I call it delicacy, a reader's weird sense of abomination. Later as I got more comfortable being around these hallways, the mere sight of the poet in the building produced in me a kind of pain.

It was not just that he was old and intermittently lucid and altered from what he may have promised to be when he wrote the poem. It was not only the mental readjustments one had to make when one saw him (continual as those adjustments were), from one's continuing historical image of him to his continuing, or may I say deconstructing, presence. The historical image, of course, receded as the present man daily peered through doors, gnashing his teeth as though chewing lifelong sheaves of paper.

It was a pain of all of these but not quite—not simply an everyman's sorrow over the passing of time, which happens to all of us, even though we are not poets.

I could not quite put my finger to it, at least not at that moment.

I had to return to the building for a class that afternoon, and I saw him again in greater shadow: the way light fell upon the day. He was in a dark hallway a bit ahead of me.

"And how did the class take it, Professor?" I asked.

"Ah, hello, hello," he said jovially, seeing but not placing me. He spoke with that jocular twang of his, peculiar to him, although they say he picked it up from his student days in the American Midwest, in Iowa with Paul Engle or Kalamazoo, amid the scent of Bienvenido Santos's apples. The Midwest was where Filipino scholars went during the Commonwealth. My own great-grandmother, Baldomera Watts, had been educated in Bloomington, Indiana, where she met the American who migrated to Tacloban, owner of MacArthur-era Botica Watts, the decrepit drugstores that have withstood floods and looting.

Professor Lector's speech was a healthy rounding of vowels, an amused adoption of a foreign language.

"Take what, my dear?"

He stopped in his tracks to wait for me near the glass entrance midway through the hall.

Light was better there.

"How did they take the fact of the death of the author?" I asked.

He put out his hands in that gesture of doubt, moving his palms up and down. "So, so," he said, shaking his head conspiratorially. "It'll take them a while to get over it."

"How long did it take you?"

I regretted that I had spoken.

Because there was this tragedy about which people whispered.

How Professor Lector had stopped writing at an age too young for everyone's wishes.

It was as much a tragedy, for some folk, as it was a mystery.

People thought they saw some signs of its cause. Knowingly they point out how after the writing of his seminal poem, Professor Lector had condemned it. He condemned the anthologizing, the commentating, and the repeated publications in Philippine journals. All of this is true. He liked the poem, he had said in an interview, but he liked others better. He pointed to his masterpiece, which the world ignored. He wrote other poems, but we continued to memorize the same lyrical relic. He grew old, but people still confronted him with his boyhood poem.

And then he had confronted them with silence. He showed them the speechlessness of his days. And it became a mystery to everyone that he spoke nothing (for when a poet publishes nothing new, he may as well be mute); when in fact, say some clever souls, when he had spoken before, readers had drowned out his words by their thoughtless applause.

That was one theory. That readers, by their early, too partial pleasure, had killed Professor Lector. The public had made him sit on his laurels, squashing them.

It's a fanciful theory.

There are others.

When I saw him in the hallways, it would sometimes seem as if his speechlessness were a long bout of self-revulsion, a cradling of an unspent loathing—"Why do I even allow myself to speak?"

But I recognized my own pale miseries in that.

He looked at me with those wide-open, humorous eyes and answered my question, which I had regretted, with that booming trill to his speech: "How long did it take me? Most of my life, my dear, most of my life. I had to teach it to myself."

· I moved on with him. We had reached his office.

"Yes," he said, frisking himself for his keys, "the author annihilates himself."

"Literally or symbolically?"

"Eternally and daily." He grinned. "That's how it should be. But mind you," he said, pointing a finger at me, "I'm not revealing any of my secrets."

He tinkered with his door's lock, as if it were difficult, but it was easily opened.

He gestured that I take a seat.

I did.

His office held the clutter of a life dwelt in the mind—books, scattered paper, college bluebooks, greeting cards from students illustrated with Virginia Woolf in facsimile smile. I suppose I sought what I hoped to find: a sign of writing in progress, his secret life that would astound skeptics and pierce the mystery once and for all.

A typewriter lay on a side table, a bulky, dusty Remington. On a sheet on his desk I quickly noted the type he favored, the merry, wide font of Pica.

"A letter to a student," he said to me. "They write me from all over, you know."

"You write them back," I said.

"Everyone. When I can, you see, when I can." He gestured to all the papers on his desk, chairs, settee, and cabinets, and upon a host of other papers and books. "They like to write to me. That's my son," he pointed to a picture. "He lives in Belgium, in Liège. Where they have these town fairs, you know—market days where they sell only guns and bullets. Can you believe it? My son lives in the world's marketplace for guns. He's a travel agent. And that's my grandchild. She plays the piano, but more spectacular than that—she drives a car. Mine! At the age of sixteen! And that's my wife."

I saw a picture of a lady in sepia. I saw calendars given by colleagues. I saw pens and penknives. I saw coffee spoons and cheery, literary mugs. But apart from the space held by the typewriter, cramped in the corner by a cabinet of books and a settee with a flowered footstool, shouldered by a calendar of wit, beginning with Oscar Wilde and downhill from there, draped with bluebooks on its keys, I failed to see his space for writing.

As if mysteries might be so easily unraveled.

And what I saw clearly was my bungling, sorry vulgarity.

Professor Lector had seated himself before me.

"Now," he said, "why are you so interested in the death of the author?"

I knew somehow he had found me out—a sneaky reader with misplaced concern. My intentions were more folly than malice, of course. I had no excuse for my spying and indecent interest but my lack of understanding.

For here was a writer whole in his world—his letters and his sons and the books he read and spoke about; a man booming with amusement in his voice, with a healthy attachment to his world—peering in through doors, taking us all in with bright, living eyes, with the penetrating, permeating voice of a midsummer's turtle.

I may have caged him in his poet's cell: I had given him only a strip of paper, long as a poem, on which to stalk and speak about things. But he had jumped out of it—he had bidden himself away from the reader.

And even when and if he did take the bluebooks off the Remington and dusted the keys to type his words in merry, fat Pica—did he have to wave the matter to the world, to the ram paging bull of readers that snorts in small circles, inhuman and impatient to see his unlifted, furled, and secret cape?

8. Fourth poetry reading

But Somerset was right: I was ripe for disillusion.

The time comes when you get tired of getting manipulated atop poem manuscripts and look for more piercing engagements. Soon I stopped visiting Sabado's flat, stopped playing chess with his father.

I was beginning to feel like one of those plants that get by on sporous reproduction.

So I looked for other modes. Sabado, as expected, did not take it as he should. He asked me to marry him. He actually bent on his left knee by his bed, took my hand and asked for it. Exactly in that way. I could see his receding hairline very clearly from that angle. In the center of his head was a bald circle, which seemed to be waiting only for some bird eggs to come forth.

I said no way.

At least, in a novel you fail to admire completely, you can still look back on some elements, a scene or two, that had made you read on. When you discuss it with others, you can point to specific passages—the wonderful paragraph on chutney, for instance, or that prologue on the grandfather's nose, which the author cleverly linked to the map of India. And you might even, despite your reservations, come to remember the book as if you had loved it entirely. In defending it to other people (simply because of your memory of some lines), you begin to find your admiration rising, as if the words you took in defending the book were helium blowing up its worth.

This was not the case with Sabado.

The more I reflected on the man, the less I desired.

It had required some skill to catch him, but much less than that to shake him off.

One finds other tilling fields. It was a fecund time for meeting poets. The country, in thrall to a dictator whose time was up, so said accountants and activists both, was finding ever more uses for community. Poetry readings, secret parties, marches, and book launchings gathered kindred souls who wished only to talk about the same thing—the president's announcement of the snap elections.

That was 1985, and the winds of change were making people sing folk songs that were driving me nuts.

Writers in different languages now found common ground. Whether English, Tagalog, Bikol, or Waray, everyone was finding hope in the smell of revolution. In private séances or public demonstrations, poets could be found clumped in congenial organizing masses.

It was wonderful finding so many authors in one fell swoop. But this also made things difficult.

I have trouble in bookstores when I arrive not knowing what I need. I get bewildered by too many choices. I'm often unable to act with dispassion. I flit from one book to another, take up three or four at a time. I lose all sense of discernment: I think each next book that I fancy must be mine. I get attached to each discovery and get mired in the mud of inarticulate priorities. I end up with a stack of books in my hand, and right until I get to the counter, I am still making my decisions. I cast some books out just as the cash register rings. I go back and retrieve others. Then I return home with this odd assortment. My bookshelf is filled with evidence of my sudden fancies and the stupid eclectic objects of my lust. Afterwards, I don't quite remember why I had brought them home.

There was Danilo, a law student who wrote villanelles. There was Carmi, short for Carmelito, who always had his epic in his pocket, ready for fond readings at odd times. There was William Howard Fortune, a mongrel like myself, who appropriately wrote doggerel. There were journalists who dabbled in terza rima, fictionists who should have remained journalists, poets-cum-painters, poets-cum-dentists, poets-cum-philanderers, admen-poets, madmen-poets, poets who rhymed and didn't, and many, many students. By then I'd learned my lesson. The best place for these matters was home.

My apartment had the advantage of being inhospitable to illusion. It was bare, small, and too sharply lit. My room had only books and a bed. My clothes were in a box in the sala. I had only one pair of shoes, a pair of open-toed sandals, which I sometimes wore even to sleep. My house's other main adornment was my toothbrush. I did everything on my bed. Ate, read, slept, fucked. Four basic functions. My sister sent me money regularly. Sometimes I forgot to pick it up. I used it so sparingly I may as well have been a pauper, eating on pork rinds when I remembered. When I thought I was in love, I couldn't eat a single thing. I lost my appetite when I most desired other things. When I found a man I wanted, I couldn't even chew rice. It was dry in my mouth. My needs were particular, recurring.

For some there was ceremony—Danilo, for instance, had a habit of brushing his teeth before and after, so that sex was like the midline of a tercet, and his habits were its uninspiring alternate rhyme. I remember fondly this young man named Felipe Rizal, whom I appropriated simply for his name (I learned later he was an actuarian who had nothing to do with the reading at all; he'd merely been a customer in the pub). This actuarian Rizal, a rather gorgeous youth of unseemly fervor, would not allow me to take off my clothes and instead sucked me through the fabric, all about my linen dress. I felt like I was being laundered in place. He, on the other hand, was naked, eager for inspection, as if seeking approval for lower life insurance premiums. He had great strategy and initiative, for a man whose name and profession, he said, always rewarded him with laughter.

One of my favorites was Fred, a cartographer who dabbled in minimalist prose. He was a spatial genius—a man with this peculiar talent: he could retain in his head self-mapped, geometric configurations of settings in different books. His stories were always inspired by the settings of other people's novels. For instance, the north-south axis of the city of Kyoto, Rashomon Gate to Rokujo Avenue in *Tale of Genji*, prompted him to write a serial tale about tricycle driver axe murderers. He was an inspired man, though his impulses were dubious. As a minimalist, he was special. He had found that all lines start with a single point, the nipple's cartographic north, and upon this he bore his considerable powers of savant-like concentration.

And then there was Jon, simple-minded as a journalist, which he was. He had less than zero appeal. I must have been drunk when I met him. No need to bore you with petty details. He had all the imagination of his craft, which in itself generates a limp derision, all the pulp of a girl's cheap pity. And yet, stet, many times he sufficed.

THE WONDERS OF torpor in a fast, disintegrating world. The way the mind reels, like raveling spool, in the wet soot of drink. And the breeze outside of cafés seems to transform, as it passes, into an ashy sweat of mind, the humid spell that comes from being too near the sea. There is that stupor in the evening. Talk has passed into a blur. What happens next is so much inevitable undoing.

There is no merit in things achieved through little striving.

It used to be I always tried to finish a book I started. I felt it was an obligation, the least I owed the writer. But like any flawed believer, I've failed too often in my vow. I've discarded more books in the middle of distraction than I care to admit.

I always looked for better prospects. Readers are an optimistic lot. There is always the next time, and the possibility of deeper, undivided attention—the book that's worth your while.

But what is it we seek?

Let me count the quests.

A shelf of bibliolepts:

1. *The Man of La Mancha*. This is the reader who believes in an ideal world as he finds it in a book.

I've always looked upon Don Quixote with the tenderness of a codependent. He is the Bibliolept In Extremis; of course, he is dysfunctional. His entire quest is a biblioleptic wound: he turned words into flesh and text into a kind of hell. Readers cannot take refuge in his absurdity. It repels and stabs us. It was right that his neighbors should put fire to his books.

Reading *Don Quixote* is like being wasted by one's own kind.

And yet one cannot help but be moved by his affliction, for the whole, indivisible universe bibliolepsy can contain.

2. *Emma Bovary*. This is the type of reader who takes a book after which to fashion her own image.

Bibliolepsy is a sign of deprivation, like scurvy or beriberi. Readers would like to live unmediated with the world, but they are afflicted by some deficiency, a rawness of expectation.

Maybe in this lay Emma's ruin.

The departure point of Emma's *pasyon* was the reading of romances. But this reader is no idealist like Quixote; she is an opportunist.

Unlike Quixote, she has no full world in her; instead, there is simply an imperfect body, a void in the bones.

This may be the most tedious kind of bibliolept: the escapist who appropriates books to patch her own face.

I am cruel about readers like Emma Bovary. But as the Frenchman said in his apocryphal dying hour—*Emma Bovary, c'est moi.*

3. *Paolo and Francesca*. For these readers, it is the book that finds them out.

The only knowledge we have of Paolo and Francesca, the lovers in Dante's hell, is that their sin had been committed by their joint reading of a story—the tale of Lancelot and Guinevere. When the kiss was sealed in the book, so was this pair's folly.

I've always felt the charm in that. How love in print begets love in the loins. I like its symmetry and idiocy. There are, of course, matters of predisposition and opportunity in the story, other crude things.

And I have always wondered about this: what had Guinevere and Lancelot read?

Readers of this sort may not even like to read at all. It's simply that one book might pander an arousal. Even so, if this happens to you, be on your guard. You are under bibilioleptic trauma.

4. *Kinbote*. The reader as scholar.

When under the feebleness of biblioleptic fever, I'd feel a serious cruelty in the critical companions to texts. Whether genial or not, dull or discerning, critical readings would assume the indelicate posture of medical knives. I would recoil.

Or, like their eponymous counterpart in *Pale Fire*, these Kinbotes come off as simply loony.

There must be a midground between articulate lunacy and speechless lust.

Under greater lucidity, I'd feed off these critical readers—lunch on them, snack on them, annotate their ruses. I might even quote them to show my full digestion of a book. I would try a bit of surgery myself, to find the space between scholarship and stupefaction.

Why are these Kinbotes necessary at all?

To legalize a drug. They are the lawyers of a reader's lust.

5. *Supremo the Reader.* This is the decisive reader who acts on a book, thus changing the course of history.

Andres Bonifacio, the Supremo of the Revolution of 1896, was a neat dresser, an autodidact, and a passionate reader. It is he, so they say, who drummed up the plot to storm an arsenal at the start of the war with Spain. His strategy was a military plot based on a novel—on the thrilling scenario in Rizal's second book, *El Filibusterismo*.

The plot failed.

Miserably.

In the book and in history.

The Supremo's immense faith in Rizal, mistaking a novel for a military manual, is also immensely touching—a kind of historical bibliolepsy that spurs legend, like Alexander the Great carrying around trunks of *The Iliad* throughout his ravage of Greece. If only it hadn't killed the Supremo's men, disheartening the revolution and making the Supremo run from the city that loved him, Manila, to that hornet's nest that killed him—Cavite.

Among all readers, I imagine him most fondly, the Supremo, misreading Rizal with fervor.

The image of a country.

6. *Bouvard and Pecuchet*. The reader as the garbage collector of culture.

This is a very common bibliolept, the one who thinks life will be improved by the books that he reads. You might say that he loves a poem for the wrong reasons, for social causes, psychology, or other misplaced solipsistic notions.

But who will bell this slippery cat, mark the limits between the right and wrong meanings?

Every reader to his own devices, fatuities, and dislocations.

For people like Bouvard and Pecuchet, let the author rant desultorily in his corner. He's simply a flea on a mightier animal. The bounding fancy of the bibliolept often stuns the wise.

LET'S CALL THE next poet Huevos Santo: Mr. Holy Eggs.

He was a huge man in a rage. I met him at the usual somnambulist's café. He had a cigarette in his mouth like a dagger. Or was that a sword in his eye? No matter. You might get the picture—hefty man, barong Tagalog, lotioned skin, and bitter sneer. He wore contact lenses. He had a gold watch. He hated readers and militants. They were his plague.

"All readers are buffoons," he told me. "And the worst buffoons are those who believe in a cause. It's best for a man not to write; but if he wrote, it's best for a man not to publish. And if he publishes, it's best for him to spit at everyone who ventures to talk about his books." And he spat smoke onto the left region of my shoulders.

"All talk is cheap," he said.

"Such as yours," I pointed out.

"And the talk of readers is the worst."

He would list to me his other woes.

"Wives, too," he told me. "I hate wives. And I hate their children."

"Then you must hate yourself," I said peaceably. "You were someone's child."

"She was no one's wife," he retorted.

Mr. Holy Eggs was a government factotum, literary force, and enormous bore. Through the years, as his influence grew larger, so had his body mass. You might say he bloated as his country declined. He was behind many of the dictator's acts of bad faith, serious injury, and malicious regard; he was one of the regime's writers and polemicists. He had his own travails—in the Byzantine tract of the dictator's court, he was sometimes favored, sometimes not. He was nobody's fool and everyone's crank. He was vicious, reptilian, and unlovable.

He deserved to be fucked over, and I did.

For those who have wondered what it is like to be saddled by a very gross man, let me tell you this: it isn't easy. Sideways or horizontal on a bed, it cannot be done. Fat overwhelms geometry. If you climbed over him, you'd simply sway. There are two ways to do it, both tricky, requiring the logistics of stamina and invention. You could do it on the edge of a bed, his body prone and yourself upright. The Kama Sutra advises you to hold tightly in a contraction known as *A Pair of Pincers*. You'd need first to ram yourself through his thighs' iron fat, in the same impossible position as Moses parting the waters. Or, failing that, you could straddle him above the thighs, gingerly holding on while you moved backwards, perpendicular to his matter.

Either way, in the room's harsh light, it was a pathetic scene. I've long figured this out: sex requires gravity, not beauty. I've been happy with men who look like horses, polliwogs, and even some creatures from other phyla. Beauty is not necessary.

It's levity that destroys desire.

And when I broke out in laughter at this beached, stripped, cacoethical marlin, this pallid ichthyosaur, Mr. Huevos Santo, who snorted to a humming in his head and displayed so nakedly some horrors of the dictatorship—the cellulite streams of dissipation, like the scars of slackened virtue, the red, tumorous folds of unchecked appetite, the fetid smell of holy balls, like the noxious gills of a very dead fish, and finally the small, tinily upright figure at the center of this squalid altar: forgive me. Faced with the state of the nation, all I could do was look down and laugh.

9. A reading of my parents' death

I did not tell Somerset of this adventure; he had worries of his own.

The predictable loss of his fourteenth entry in the Palanca Memorial Literature Awards did not at all move him. He'd come to expect that as part of his fate, a fixed ritual, like planetary motion.

No, he was concerned about an ominous change.

He returned from Makati one day in a state of panic.

"Have you seen what they're doing out there?" he asked us.

I was with his wife Margaret, nicknamed May, a woman of many virtues, the least of them being that she was filthy rich.

"Filing their fingernails?" I asked. "What do Makati office girls do, May?"

"Order lunch," she said. She returned to her book.

May was a rotund woman with a Joycean obsession. She had fallen in love with Somerset because, she said, he was a writer with a vague look of blindness.

Her book was another memoir by a man who knew James Joyce when he had been depressed in Zurich or singing Irish rebel songs in Trieste. It was by his optician or his wife's gynecologist.

"No." Somerset was red in the face. He took a seat and wiped his brow. "They're throwing bits of phone paper all over the streets."

May looked up brightly. She closed her book. "Oh yes. That. Isn't it wonderful?"

"What?" I asked. I took May's book from her. She said she'd lend it to me the minute she was done. She'd reached the part where the gynecologist—or was it Nora's beautician?—was expounding on his own anatomical contribution to a short line in *Finnegans Wake*.

"Don't you know, Primi? Are you so out of touch that you don't know what they are doing on the streets of the city, how times are changing?" May was a bit put out.

"No, they're not, May," said Somerset vigorously. "Times are not going to change because of a few shredded phone books. Not in my lifetime."

"Oh, that," I said. "Yeah. The last time I saw my sister, that's all she talked about."

"You have a sister?" asked May.

"Why do you look so surprised? Yes, I do."

"Where is she?" May asked. "I thought you were an orphan."

"I am," I said. "But there are two orphans in my family. She's a healer. In Banahaw."

"A healer?"

"A mystic," I volunteered. I thought I might as well reveal the rest. "She's changed very much since she was a child. Actually, she had been a very strange child. She became different—but still perhaps strange—when she decided to live on the mountain. She discovered she has a gift of prophecy." I shrugged my shoulders.

"Really? Your sister? What's her name?"

"Anna," I said. "Anna Valenzuela."

May and Somerset looked at each other. Somerset groaned.

"Anna Valenzuela is your sister?" May almost squeaked.

"Yes," I said. "Do you know her?"

"She's our group's prayer leader. Somerset, what a coincidence."

"Yes, yes," Somerset said impatiently, still musing on his vision of Makati. "How will my fiction ever be able to withstand this—if our country is taken over by a revolution of Makati *matronas?*"

He shook his head and buried his face in his arms.

I HAD BROUGHT my gift of tamarinds on that scheduled date with Anna. When the Abuelita died, Anna had become my sole guardian and the executor of my grandmother's wealth, or what was left of it—the dregs of the Abuelita's long senility. Anna regularly sent me money by post. Occasionally, we'd see each other: usually on the day of my parents' wedding anniversary (which had also been the day of my grandfather's death, seven months before Anna was born).

We had agreed to meet the day I was looking for Sabado's books, and despite my frenzy on that week, we did see each other at a café on UN Avenue, full of Italian food and Filipino flies. There were office workers and students in the café, as well as a couple of foreign tourists, each with many splotches on their greasy faces, as if they had been sprinkled by wayward mites from the same bin, victims of love or mosquito bites. Everyone, tourists and women, bankers and students, shifted their angle of vision when Anna walked in. It's incredible what a beautiful woman can do to a room, the way a stage moves naturally to her corner, so that the configurations change. She creates the room's angles, its periphery and spotlight.

Anna wore sunglasses, flowing white trousers, and a white shirt. She carried a rattan backpack and took a while to shake it off. Her hair was long, waving carelessly about her shoulders. Her smooth face was suntanned to a nectarine pitch: she had my mother's ability to redden, but my father's slow burn.

She was just twenty-seven and had already been through two husbands. She was on her way to becoming a diwata, a healer, a mountain goddess, all on her own.

The mountain people loved her. In Banahaw, she carved little gods out of mountain stone as big as her thumbnail. She had the ability to weave intricate doilies out of talahib. On the backs of the mountain people, she could create the marvelous creatures of their fantasy—wise old men with fading beards, voluptuous deities with river-like hair, Elvis Presley as someone had prophesied he would die: with jewels around his body already like the studs on a porphyrian tomb. She could illustrate these with her needles or even just her hands.

I remember when she used to draw miniature kangaroos, imitating the images on paperback spines, onto her toenails, or whittle entire miniature playgrounds out of a matchbox with her deft fingers.

Her fingers were like Prospero's: she had a gift.

People preferred, in fact, the drawings she created by the pressure of her fingertips. They were invisible to everyone but the person on which the drawings were bestowed—the lucky persons walked about with the impression of a god only they could configure and their flesh could trace. This impression could last for days. The longest had lasted three weeks, but Anna believed the man was a liar. He wanted to impress her with his sensitivity.

She possessed my father's artistry and my mother's beauty. And Anna had achieved her childhood miniaturist's dreams, in more ways than one.

As for me, all I had gotten were my father's sullenness, a misplaced aptitude for a foreign language, and odd peripatetic habits, which perhaps my mother would have understood.

When Anna reached my table, she shook her head at me.

As I looked at her, I again wondered at it: how startlingly she looked like our mother.

I could almost see Prima gazing at me as if at a disfigured animal, doubtful of its possibilities.

I stood up to kiss her. She stooped down to hug me, holding me so tightly I thought I would lose hearing, if not air.

When she let me go, she sat down. She shook her head again at me.

"Oh Primi, Primi. Your aura is so dirty," she said, continuing to move her head from side to side and looking at a line above my brow. "It's so orange. All cloudy like jeepney dust, do you see it? So thickly cloudy. Like the color of tuba, and not the bahalina kind. What are you doing to yourself?"

"Nothing," I said. "I'm in college. I have new friends."

"You should have come with me to Banahaw. I should have made you go. School is no place for a growing girl. Look at you. At least your aura had some light blue before, with faint yellow only because you were so sickly, always puking up. But you have changed so much. You are sleeping with ugly men."

I had to nod.

"You're not fulfilling your potential." Anna sighed.

A waiter hovered by her side, but she didn't notice him.

She combed a hand through her hair then reached over to touch my brow. "You could have grown into a vivid blue," she said solemnly, leaning her face toward me. I wished she would whisper, not talk so loud. Her face was only inches from mine. "Like the sky in the morning when you can't tell it from the sea. Or at least you could have become a little silvery, like a dolphin's fin. Primi: between the two of us, it is you who had the potential for goodness."

I was used to my sister's arrivals. Intensity seven on some scales.

The waiter stayed with us, paper and pen in hand. He stood as if mesmerized by my sister.

I looked down and tried to squirm away.

"Why?" I asked.

She had actually told me this before. What she had thought

I would become. Before she had left the poet Joaquin in Ermita, she had analyzed briefly the differences between our fates.

She sat back into her seat.

"Because I was always an unhappy child," Anna again smugly explained to me. "You were more obedient. You were more content, sitting with your books. You know how I fought every stupid thing in the world, the Abuelita, my teachers—"

"And mine, too," I added.

"My husband, my other one, all those moronic men who were in fact offering me some kind of love, if you think about it. I fought every form of love people are able to give. I couldn't accept it."

"You used your beauty to contain your needs," I said.

Anna nodded.

I had heard that before.

Before she had become a mystic, she had been to a psychotherapist.

On one occasion, she had dragged me with her.

"You were orange," I said, as if these clunky analyses were my duty.

It struck me again how disappointed I was in growing up when I saw my sister Anna—she used to unleash her enormous energy in reckless disdain. Since going up the mountain, she had become this flipside of her person—you could sense her pent strength, but now it was driven by a confusing mysticism, equal in fervor to her old rage.

She looked at me ruefully. "I guess I was. You know I really did think I loved Joaquin. I thought: here was a man whose gentleness and intelligence I could live with. You remember how he used to recite poetry all the time. Riding through a mountain range, taking a bus. He could recite works of poets, mostly Germans, right off the top of his head. Lyrical words to fit every occasion. Well, that drove me nuts! I couldn't concentrate on the scenery if I had a poem whispering in my goddamned ear. I couldn't breathe if too many words interfered. He made me hate books even more than I already did."

"Yes," I said. "You told me that. But, Anna, you know. You're the best reader I've ever met."

When we were children, she could analyze Kafka like a blizzard cutting through air.

Anna continued: "I haven't read a book or a newspaper since I left him."

"Really?"

"Reading makes your aura turn gray. Dull and inert. You need the mountain air, the scenery of the woods to make you healthy. Would you like to go up Banahaw again?"

"Not really," I said.

"I knew you wouldn't. Anyway, I'm moving for a while into the city."

"I thought that would mess up your aura."

"The city needs me," she said gravely.

"Are you serious?"

"It's been prophesied."

"What?"

"With prayer we can turn the tide. This is the year."

"The year for what?"

"Primi, this is the year the country will change. Haven't you noticed? People are moving. Forces are coming together. With that energy exploded from the death of the prophet—"

"Who? Ninoy Aquino? The senator who died on that airport tarmac three years ago?"

My sister nodded.

"I thought he was simply comprador burgis who got unlucky. Or lucky, depending on how you look at it. He wasn't even a revolutionary," I said.

"He's one of the prophets. His coming was a sign."

"Of his doom, certainly. He died! They killed him! Just like that. He came off the plane to fight the beasts, and the monsters killed him, blaming it on that sad lone gunman, Rolando Galman, who died in his underwear and never lived to tell the story. Come on, Anna. This country is doomed. Ronald Reagan will never let his great friend Ferdinand Marcos fall. They're twins. Or at least one is his puppy, the other is his master. That's what the radicals say, I mean, the kids in the dorms."

"Don't you notice the change in the country? In the mountains, for instance, there are a bunch of cloud formations that repeat themselves. They have repeated these patterns continually the past three years, since the prophet died."

"What do they look like? I once saw Franz Kafka in a cloud. I looked at his image again, and he began to look like Frida Kahlo."

"Don't be facetious. The clouds are shaped like buildings, like swarms of people and buildings."

"That's simple television, Anna. That's what you see on television. The confetti crowd. Office workers and businessmen and accountants raining the yellow pages on student protesters in solidarity. The yellow ones are out there daily on the buildings, strewing bits of phone paper from their windows. It's a strange form of protest, at any rate. This Yellow Revolution. I don't see how they're going to kick him out with phone paper and marching demonstrations. And besides, clouds always look like crowds. And buildings, too."

Anna smiled, shaking her head.

She noticed the waiter then and ordered mineral water. I ordered pizza, sourbread, and a Coke.

"Primi, you've regressed. You've simply become a skeptic. Not even mom turned into that."

I kept quiet.

She kept quiet.

"It's unfair to bring up Prima," I said finally. "Neither of us knew her well enough to tell."

"Primi, I hate to say this—"

"Yeah, I know." I repeated the mantra. "You'll always be seven years older than I. But still, you were only fourteen when she died."

"How do you know that she died?"

"Anna, are you going nuts?"

"We never saw her body. We don't know if she died."

"That is just plain crazy. The mountain air might be nice for your constitution, Anna, but I'm sorry to say it's not doing well for your brains."

Anna laughed out loud. And even laughing she was beautiful. I had to smile at my sister.

"Seriously, Primi. I've never believed Prospero or Prima were dead. I didn't see them die."

I sat still, staring. I watched my sister in her unruly, flagrant loveliness. I looked to see if there were features in her I'd over-looked, which had become unrecognizable, alien. But she looked as I'd always known her: a reincarnation of my mother.

"No one saw them die," Anna continued, turning even redder as she did when she was earnest. "We never buried their bodies. They might have transformed themselves, for all we know. They might be some different resurrected creature we still need to look out for. Remember, mother was always talking about that. Resurrection. It's all in her journals."

"The Authentic Resister," I said. "I've always wondered what she meant by that."

Anna at first didn't answer.

"You didn't know? Ah well, you were only seven."

"Eight," I corrected. "What should I know?"

The Authentic Resister had been a figure in my mother's

journals, a person or creature that she sought for reasons of taxidermy, I had imagined.

"Ask Uncle Diego. He'd be able to explain."

"No. You tell me."

"Prospero and Prima were rebels. It's that simple."

"Against what?"

"The regime, dummy. They were authentic resisters. They killed themselves in 1972, when you were eight—seven, really, because you were born in December. It was the year and month martial law was declared. Haven't you figured that out?"

"I thought it was—well, I always thought it had something to do with dolphins. Or something. Or maybe they just wanted to leave us. They were tired of us."

"That's what I thought, too. For the longest time. But Uncle Diego gave me these. Remember?" And Anna took out what she had in her bag.

They were sheaves of cartoon strips, folded and bent by the shape of her bag. They were entitled *Anibal the Ipis, a Patriotic Cartoon*. In them were the heads, arms, legs, and wings of a cockroach in different poses of suffering and stubbornness.

"These are the last things he had sent Uncle Diego," Anna said. "He had made these for a contest. But he didn't win."

"He killed himself because he didn't win a contest?"

"No, no. I don't think so. The regime was his sorrow. Can't you see? Mother was a taxidermist—her obsession was death. It was all the same to her whether they lived or died."

"That's a rather catch-all theory," I said.

I looked at the cartoons. They were yellow, wrinkled, and extraordinary. In my memory, I had always thought of my father, in his last days, writing a book of extremities documenting the poses of love—the coital mouth, the attitudes of passion. Do I shade in my remembrances with my own wishes, like a cartoonist with a wayward will? Instead, he had been drafting a storyboard for a nationalist rag.

I held the drawings with what seemed the dawning of hunger, long ignored.

"I'd like to give these to you," Anna said. "I will be moving around too much. I can't take care of them. I think I've seen her, you know."

I looked up.

Anna took her water from the waiter. My pizza was soggy and sweet. I couldn't eat it. I couldn't chew.

"Who do you mean? You've seen whom?"

"Well. I haven't seen Prima, really. Not yet. But I have smelled her."

"Don't tell me it's a fortune flower," I said.

"It is, yes," said Anna with surprise. "How did you know?"

"Anna, we went through this before. Remember I told you that long ago when you went on your hunger strike, everyone believed the ghost of mother was in her room and it was really just a fortune flower? The scent pervaded the entire house."

"You know, I don't remember that," Anna said. "I don't remember your saying it was a fortune flower."

"Maybe it wasn't."

I was beginning to be confused. I tried again to eat, but I couldn't.

"I remember the smell in my room when I went on strike," Anna said. She did not look at me. She looked at her hands, contemplating limbs, wrists. "I've carried it with me everywhere I've gone. I hold it right here. I try to think of this scent when I don't feel right. Its memory protects me."

I didn't speak.

"You know, I remember that hunger strike as clearly as if it had happened—as if it had happened just now. All throughout, while I lay on the bed, I smelled that scent of a flower. It was what I thought something godlike would be. I had always liked those myths. The stories of the gods. Resurrection. Nectar. Myrrh, ambrosia, frankincense. I knew I wouldn't die if the smell remained. Then it disappeared."

"Yes, Anna, you collapsed."

"No," she said. "The smell withdrew. And I've been looking for it since. All over Banahaw." Absently, she speared my pizza with my fork. I pushed the plate toward her. "And you know," she said, chewing on the dough, looking at me, "I think I found it. I found mother's scent on the mountain. I believe she'll show herself to me. Soon. Any day now, she'll reappear."

Looking at my sister slowly savoring that pizza, her lips greasing up, I felt I couldn't take in what she was saying.

"Anyway, what I believe is that Prospero and Prima are part of the forces moving the country. Mystical forces, forces of nature. You know it is no coincidence that I copied my hunger strike from the hunger strike of that prisoner, Ninoy Aquino, in 1972?"

"So he was the same one in the news then, the prisoner fasting against martial law?"

"You think it is a coincidence that my visions are now coming to fruition? Oh Primi. Don't you think father would be one of the first in line at these demonstrations, if he were alive? Remember how his robots were banned, *Voltes V,* how outraged he was by the dictator's decree about the television show?"

"No," I said. "The show was banned years after his death, Anna."

"Remember how he and Diego would discuss politics way into the night, the way kids and people were disappearing from Leyte and Samar—do you remember their concern about the war in the countryside?"

"No, Anna." I looked away from my sister, from the thoughts that occurred to me as she spoke. I felt a spread of goose bumps, like repressed tears, prickle through my skin. "I don't remember that at all. I remember that they liked to recite Filipino poets through the night, like a duel. Jose Garcia Villa. Versus everyone else."

"You and your childish, selective memory." Anna laughed. Light played about her marble face. "We each have our ways, Primi. Anyway, we must heed these forces. If enough people gather together to pray long enough and hard enough, creating a mass of positive energy, it will happen."

"What?"

"The dictator will leave. Prima and Prospero will be avenged."

"How do those two different things go together?"

Anna sighed, then sipped her drink, breathing in fully. When she was done she said: "Primi, you will always be seven years younger than I."

10. Miercoles Santo

Somerset's head remained nestled in his arms.

"He can't stand the prospect of a happy reversal," May said to me matter-of-factly. "He refuses to join me in my prayer group. He thinks we are mystics with no foresight, optimists without erudition. He says we have no sense of history. Just banal hope. But change has happened before in less than auspicious forms. There's the American Revolution, started by tax-evading tea drinkers. Though on second thought, look what that brought them—imperialist scum! Anyway, why can't our own be papered by the yellow crowd of office workers? It's an argument against the yellow crowd that they are, in many cases, counterrevolutionary—but we must take momentum where we can. Somerset prefers his nihilism only because it allows him to write."

"May, I will drive you to your prayer group. What else do you want? I just can't see things changing by mere wishing."

"It's not wishing, Somerset. We are acting. We are all players in this plot—it's just that everyone does things in different ways. You, for instance, prefer to stick your neck in the sand."

"I do not."

May said to me: "Somerset did not even vote for Cory Aquino, you know. He's with that boycott-the-election crowd. He and the wild lefties remain in their mad embrace with the dictator—they can't let each other go. Well, I prefer to march—and pray for the best."

"What would James Joyce do?" I asked her.

"He would say: 'Welcome, O life! I go to encounter for the millionth time the reality of experience and forge in the smithy of my soul—'"

Somerset closed his hands over his ears.

May and I couldn't help laughing at the sight of him.

"What about you, Primi," she said. "Would you like to join me? When did you last see your sister?"

"Not recently," I said. Instinctively, I reached to touch the top of my head, as if I might feel my crown of orange silt. "What do you do?"

"We gather together to create a mass of positive energy. Scientists have discovered new things about prayer."

"Science? It's been researched?" I asked.

"Yes. Most possibly prayer creates low-frequency electromagnetic signals that physically effect change."

"I'm sure Einstein discovered that equation," Somerset muttered.

"Don't listen to him. Marcos's prison damaged his soul," May told me.

"That's no wonder," I said.

May waved away my irrelevant comment. "Well, anyway, we march and join the campaign for Cory's presidency, too: but we also gather every evening to pray. It's happening all around the city. It's not a Christian thing: not at all. We're not all Catholics. At least I am not. But we believe in the natural power of the universe to heal itself. It only takes a concentrated thought. And your sister Anna is one of our leaders. You know, you look like her. Now I see it."

May inspected me closely.

"I can see a vague resemblance. But you have none of her blinding, white aura: yours is orange."

LATER THAT EVENING, we arrived at a house in Cubao. Somerset drove us.

It was not his idea of dialectical combat.

It was not my sort of arena.

It was a bare, unfinished duplex whose cement walls were painted in a single, flimsy layer of white: the building's gray underskin soaked like a stain through its watery dye. The first person I met, a flaccid though bulging man with thinning hair, welcomed me with the air of desultory keep that plastered the house—a strap of a sleeveless cotton sando fell from his spotty left shoulder as he waved me in. His face was gray and mottled, like the speckled, rotting inner skin of a dead cat.

"Come on in," he intoned blankly in a familiar voice.

I could not place him, but it seemed I'd seen him before.

I recognized several women in the place. They had recited poems at a Protest Reading at the Park. I recognized the woman who had been in a batik suit and now wore a caftan. The woman who had been in a caftan now wore batik. I smiled at a girl in cat's-eye glasses who carried a cigarette but did not light it. Smoking was not allowed in this windowless place of prayer without a fire exit. Cat's-Eye smiled back at me. The gathered women of the house each had her own proper look of preoccupation, but each glance invited outsiders with that spreading locus of sympathy, abstract and distant, that mothers and physicians might have. They were standing, or sitting in lotus position, talking in pairs and threes. There were some men in collared shirts, one gray man with a pipe. I recognized Sabado among the believers. He was wearing his white shirt, and his back was to me. I could see the curling dip of his glasses' hook tucked over a fleshy, hair-filled ear.

I turned around to sidestep an unfortunate reunion. Facing the open door, I saw Anna come in.

"Primi," she said, smiling with genuine surprise. She wore a white straw hat. It was always a surprise to recognize how much I missed her when I saw her. "I knew I'd see you here sometime. I'm so glad you're here."

And she hugged me close.

She felt fevered, as she often did.

She introduced me to May. "This is my little sister."

"May brought me here," I informed Anna.

Anna nodded: "That's wonderful." To me, she said: "Primi, all you need to do is center on your inner core—don't fidget, and you'll be fine. Did you get your allowance?"

"Yes."

"Liar. You haven't touched your bank account in two months. How in hell do you eat?"

"Anna, I'm not just your little sister anymore. You don't have to watch over me."

"How can I not, Primi? You're the only family I have."

Before I could speak, the man in the sando came to Anna and took her away to an inner room.

Other people arrived. A swell of people with gravid eyes settled into place without being told. We made a circle, then a spiral so we might fit. We each had a hand upon a person next to us. Someone had turned on two standing fans I hadn't noticed. Behind us, pushed against the wall, were a smatter of wooden furniture, a desk, and two child-size chairs.

The man in the sando began.

Once he spoke, I recognized him. He was the bookseller who had sold me Sabado's two volumes. I had not been able to reconcile the blunt man in the bookstore with this broad, supplicating face. Amid books, he had seemed sharp-eyed, even acerbic. I remembered how he had stacked his wares. By his dry opinion of them. But amid the praying crowd, he lost his angles and glint, his shape unfocused.

It was the effect of a contemplation from which I was barred.

When he spoke, he reminded me clearly of who he was. He had a distinct Mandarin accent, guttural tonalities and errant grace: there was that lilt in his tone, musical and confusing. As I strained to figure out what he was saying, I met Sabado's eye. He nodded at me. I smiled back. We both returned to the holiness at hand.

"Before we begin, first we must try to touch the soul. For this, we must desire to achieve intuitive understanding. Let us try this exercise: Close your eyes. Sense within yourself the source of power in your lungs, your diaphragm, your body. Follow this power moving outward through your entire being, through the mouth and throat, through your arms and toes, through the pores of your body, through your esophagus and guts, bile and bones, fluids and flesh and fingertips, moving in all directions. But you are the center. Imagine this flow moving, reaching then through the walls of this house and the streets of this city, through the countryside and clouds, extending through Manila Bay and toward the world."

I tried to do that, but trying to figure out his words blocked concentration. I looked at Sabado, who seemed to be laughing.

I watched people. Eyes were pressed tight in a keen practice of devotion. Everyone seemed to be waiting to expel some surprising gust of air. May had a calm, contented expression, as if the red motes that wander in one's eye were dancing along some particularly tranquil screen in hers. As instructed, I tried to find my own center, the deep glow of being.

But I do not have a capacity for automatic rumination.

I must be turned by a key.

Next, it was Anna's turn to lead.

Someone placed a plastic basin in front of her, the width of the table. It held shallow water.

"Now we shall concentrate on our city. What is it that I see?" And she peered into the blue-colored basin, head stiffened before its reflection.

She said:

"A long stretch of road

Not of stones and gravel

But of people

A number in the millions

and a day on the twenty-fourth.

A color: red, but yellow, too,

victory in peace, peace in victory.

Our day has come, and a star will lead us.

Let us think of our city. Victory in peace and peace in victory. Close your eyes."

They did.

Anna had become Nostradamus with a plastic bowl, Cassandra with a bandehado. I could not take it in.

I could see a duplicitous image—Anna as she was and Anna as she had been. While she spoke, she kept niggling at her hair, teasing it into curls: that had always been her habit. Even as a prophetess, she retained some odd gestures of a child. She would tuck her lip in, for instance, to signify punctuation. She scratched her thigh inelegantly, lifting the long, white cotton of her robes. She had a tendency, whenever she looked at me, to smile broadly, the way she used to when we would share by our glances the secret of our tedium in Tacloban's public rites, at Santo Niño church.

At the same time, she continued her incantatory speech.

I looked at faces, inspected their poses of concentration.

Meditation was not good for me. It made me think too deeply of the physical space we occupied between us.

Instead, it's elsewhere that I have found proper communion and an embodiment of contemplation.

This is what I'd look for in a book.

I looked at Sabado. You may find my responsorial psalm extraordinary—this wayward reaction to prayer.

It was much later that night when it became clear Sabado had no surprises to offer me. Alone, we found ourselves in the midst of a tale—the moribund Wednesday of the week—in the derelict compromise that sometimes satisfies. We each took our positions, mouth on prick and cunt in hand. It was the symmetry of the middle ground, of lovers neither lost nor found.

11. Fat Tuesday

The country was in the mood for massive demonstrations. One couldn't single out just one mardi gras, but a whole series of them, a virtual train of linked multiple orgasmic feats, rippling through metropolis and islands like a prolonged shuddering of bulls. There had been the declaration of the widow's candidacy, Cory Aquino of the Yellow Crowds, late in the year. Then the chain of prayer rallies and counter-rallies (smaller and more specious). Then the boycott rallies of February, 1986, after the elections, when the dictator won, of course, and crowds condemned the regime's fraud by refusing to buy tainted regime goods, San Miguel Beer and such. In the midst of this there were the little clitoral sparks among parts of the city, prayer groups or small, organized marches that commemorated one hero here, another there. There was an ongoing orgy of wrath, optimism, and denunciation. The country lay within a steady fever, buoyed by quick repeated thrusts of giddiness at one point, pain and horror the next. May, for instance, shuttled between hope and a recurring desolation, which perhaps, she said, one could more easily bear.

Where was I? May and Somerset would deliver me to these rallies. Sometimes, they brought Anna along, and a whole slew of articulate mystics, knowledgeable of the many different meanings of events and the shapes of clouds. Chiefly, at these events we drank juice through a straw in Tetrapak and applauded many microphone-damaged harangues. We were there to show our bodies. To be counted among the millions. That, we believed, was the least one could do.

"I was for boycotting the election myself," Somerset would tell me, "but hey, it's a free country."

And he'd clap and sing the favored song.

Gathered here and there by friends and well-meaning sister, I would pause fitfully when allowed to take my breath, and I'd retreat to the school library.

My country had become an increasingly tellable tale. That is, if one tried to recapitulate events, they were, quite easily, an ordered, rising Freitag's triangle, with rising action, climax, and decipherable denouement—an end that could go one way (epic grace) or another (tragic fall).

It's not easy to live within a novel. One wishes to tear out from the inevitability of the plot line to rehearse the uniqueness of one's voice. One does not wish to lie awash, willy nilly, within the commanding stream of another's story. I've felt sometimes, in these many stories I've read, a character's wish to drop anchor—right as the story is getting interesting—and get up from the page and pluck hair from her armpits or clean out her navel, something totally elemental and gross: something beyond her author's eye.

Just as, in this wind-rushed tale of 1986, I'd felt a need to move out from under fate's fast-moving pen, scribbling along so surely, tilt-wise, across the span of our normal lives—to jump off history's inexorably written text, the truck of time, and fall into a ravine of my own choosing. A vagabond from history, a runaway from time. Such is the promise of sex and love—and the readings that go with them: the thrill of a moment's stalled flesh, while the rest of the world whizzes by.

• • •

IT WAS AT this point that I met these penultimate boys.

One was Manuel Misericordia.

For all of you taken by his sneering power—don't worry. I have nothing unworthy to say about him.

I met him where many others must have seen him and snickered—at one of those protest poetry readings, in which he stood apart from a crowd of placard-waving essayists denouncing Marcosian tactics in split infinitives.

He had long wild hair and a scar on his cheek.

He was called, in protest circles, a war freak and an adventurist. He loved lightning rallies and tear gas. He was a sucker for water cannons and always carried upon his bag a patch of the guerrilla flag, with the Kalashnikov salient in its field.

"It's one damned pajama party," Manuel said to me.

I was looking at his figure, trying to penetrate his aura. Beset on all sides by magicians of different sorts—wordsmiths and psychics— I thought I might as well practice, modestly and on my own, what limited skills I had on certain men.

I had just been reading Manuel in a book of what people called "committed" poetry, a notion that, in fact, had the savor of asylums or at least the mildly disturbed. But they were, of course, poems about a single theme, nationalism along different scales of hysteria.

I decided I liked Manuel best because he was direct and particularly vicious, one might say overachieving, in his rage over the doings of the dictatorship. He was said to write prose in poetry, whatever is meant by that—meaty perorations in twisted syntax. But amid the dense structures, you'd strangely find sudden clarity— as in a cougher finding soothing yet perplexing relief in the lungs after an extended bout of hapless wheezing. You remembered his poems for these single compact declaratives of sheer vitriol.

"Scum of my anus and pus in my balls," went a less successful poem of his about some notable government lout.

His prose style, I believe, had earned him some years in prison.

"A damned slam book party," Manuel hissed at me.

"What do you mean?" I asked.

"Do you like this stuff?" he asked me, waving his hand about the audience applauding the next poet, who was reading with clenched fist.

"We all come here in good faith," I told him.

"That's all right for churches," Manuel said. "Is it healthy for the brain? To be quite honest, I am uncomfortable at gatherings where everyone is pretty certain of everyone else's opinion. At least," he added, "they could stop distributing this damned Tet- rapak and give us some beer."

"It's under boycott," I said.

"Damn these yellow-shirted, teetotaling, martyr wannabes."

"It's your turn," I said to him. "They're calling your name."

IN TRUTH, MY time with Manuel's aura was a failure—I never got closer to him than at that moment. I had to give up psychic measures altogether. He was faithful to a girlfriend who had been with him through thick and thin, a fellow rebel of a fiery cause, who, so they say, had recently fled to the mountains, to the communists, and left him, more faithful to the war than to him.

NOW THIS LAST-MENTIONED boy had the lilting name of Soñador.

By itself, the key turns again, and I watch myself in activity with this man in the swelter of those orgiastic times. Fernando Soñador was a major in music, minor in philosophy. He was a student of writing but quit when he found a suitable lament for his disgust.

"Why study it," he said with adorable scorn. "Did Leo Tolstoy take a course in creative writing? Did Nick Joaquin? Did Anne Sexton?"

"Actually," I said, "she did."

"At any rate, it is utterly silly to be sitting in a class talking about writing, if you can in fact be in your own room doing it. I don't understand this waste of time."

I didn't either. I barely listened to his tirade. Its half-chewed truths fell off me as if I were deaf, because Fernando was an intolerably beautiful man. As I said, I can live with monstrosity and plainness—but beauty has its own obvious rewards.

He wouldn't take off even his jacket, and what could a decent girl do?

There would sometimes be idle moments between protest demonstrations.

In February, I used to see him at school driving his motorcycle, books strapped to the back: Heidegger and Haydn, Arcellana and Alfón—the come-ons of proper nouns. Fernando himself was an overwhelming sight: a curly-haired wanness feeding gluttony. On the library steps, I would wait for him to stop. His bike was always parked near the covered walk beside the building. I used to watch and wait for it although I didn't know him.

It may have been because of the season's direct simmer—we were often the only ones at the stacks. Everyone else was preoccupied with the confetti-and-finger-waving war.

But first let me explain the nature of that place.

The stacks in the university's main library are a stage set of an unnamable trope for fancy.

You need permission to enter. It is sealed off from the rest of the sections. It is dreaded by the simple. It is unknown to fools. It is the secret lair of bibliolepts, a refuge for solitude and exhumation, a way of revealing and of hiding.

You imagine it, in memory, as meshed in dark angles and alternate shafts of light. A minor labyrinth of intermittent arousal. For that is what occurs as you pass through.

The books here are those less commonly used, or of rarer edition, or simply of diminished shape. It's a trash bin and a museum, a recondite passion and an obvious place for trysts. Some books that are marked for the stacks are just not there at all. That means then that they are totally irrecoverable. They will never return to the world. Some books you find exactly where you expect them.

Some books you come upon through strategy, destiny, or simple cumulative observation.

I knew the books Fernando looked for, Russian fictionists and German poets. I'd stand around. If he were looking at Paul Celan, I'd be beside Chekhov.

It was a natural twist of fate.

And there was the Sunken Garden, ready for my conclusion. Down in the Garden we sank. It was all too easy to turn motorcycle, spume and chrome and sweat-of-leather. Soñador was true to his name: he looked over me as if dreaming. There was time in that instance to work on his jacket and unzip.

Down in the Garden, orificial slope between the library and Vinzons Hall, we lay in our mandibular green. In the daytime, it's where soccer players play, the Latagaw Club hosts its horse shows, and children fly kites in March. This idyll leaves ghosts in the goalposts shadow feet guard, in the sharp wind of open night space moving against absent strings of children's kites. The emptiness sings. Tracks of people and animals sink in the bending grass, and brown patches shape the sizes of booths even when the Fair is out of season. Notions of life remain in this unmanned space, and even now the imprint of Fernando's length might betray itself near the library path. Leave the path and come upon the distraction of trees on the fringes of the green, move just a bit beyond into the shadows the trees cast and watch our funny figures grasp and grope in the grass like monads grappling with indissoluble absolute selves.

Several people watched. In fact, it was a possible stampede of people, coeds, doctoral candidates, a drunk physicist, a land surveyor taking up law, several astonished engineering students with only a thesis left before they received their master's, and two security guards from the Ipil-Ipil dorm.

It was the last, a female guard with mildly eczematic skin, Mana Tarcing Bugho, also my friendly neighbor in Area Six, who glared her flashlight onto our faces. Luckily for Fernando he was a modest boy: he hadn't even allowed me to take off his shirt. Luckily for us we had chosen the missionary path: otherwise, I cannot vouch for what may have been seen.

So it came to pass that Fernando and I had been the lone duo on the grass on the night of the last, prolonged mardi gras: the eve of the defection of the minister and the general, February 22, 1986, when the entire Ipil-Ipil dorm roused themselves to fortify democracy, marching toward the street of Epifanio de los Santos Avenue, or EDSA as it is now mythologized—finding on their way these sunken souls in the Sunken Garden. What shame.

Now Fernando: dream on.

12. Catalepsy

The chain of protests, like the minute catenae of clitoral pleasure, swelled into the wave of this climax—which, in fact, was a matter of waiting, even of calm.

Catalepsy is the word that comes to mind. Days of suspended animation. In the cataleptic state, limbs remain in the pose in which they had succumbed to shock. So did the nation.

I would like to say that upon hearing the news, Fernando and I immediately put on what we'd discarded of our clothes and sped to EDSA.

I am sorry to say it was not so. We moved on to my room in Area Six.

I'd easily let history pass me by if I had a warm hand on my cunt every morning.

That was my sorry admission to the doctor who wished to cure me of my ways.

"Don't you think that's a bit shortsighted?" she said.

My doctor was a trim woman in a sleek Makati office. My problem perplexed her.

I tried to explain—the luxury of waking up daily to the softness of a hand beside me, the way males revert to neoteny, the idiocy of childhood, in their sleep. I described to her the sight: the way so many of them protect themselves like vestal virgins— as their private parts visibly dream, their hands are carelessly upon them.

I told her of Prima, my mother's restiveness: was it this that drove her to the sea—my father's slumber, the way sleep seemed to be its own life form, a quality of Being separate from the man? How is one to deal altogether with the individual's terrible isolation, gathered in sleep?

"But why should it always have to do with writers? And why can you not put it in its proper place? And why should it be so episodic or serial?"

"I don't know," I said. "I thought I came here to ask you that."

EACH SLEEP SEEMS like the postscript of a stranger—and yet there is the hand on the labia, his curls upon my breast. I barely knew the man I woke up to—Fernando was less forthcoming than most.

In the daylight, my apartment looks even more frighteningly like the cell of a lazy, negligent ascetic. Space is constricted further by the box of clothes in the bare living room; space is made emphatic by the leaning toothbrushes by the sink; books strewn all over the floor narrow the remaining emptiness.

Fernando took cups and made coffee. He washed dishes, wiped them, and set the table. He brushed his teeth with a brush he always carried on him, as he explained. And all the while as he moved, he picked up books. He took them up one by one, so that by the time he had called me over to the table, he had a bundle in his arm, held awkwardly, like uneasy children.

He laid them before him and at table talked only of my books, testing my responses to certain names as if he held a barometer. This was how we spent the morning of the first day of the revolt. We measured ourselves on biblioleptic scales. We reviewed the books before us, publishers, paper quality, and sturdiness of spines. We found we both had a passion for 5-cent Pocket Books that now sold for five bucks, and skinny, yellow-leaved Bantams with psychedelic cover scripts that had nothing to do with the sedate canonical lives within them.

But when I asked him about his own life, he changed the subject.

He had nothing to share with me but books.

That exasperated me.

"Is that all you can talk about?"

"Yes," he said.

What was strange, I told the doctor, was this. On that morning, that did not charm me.

Whether it was the time or boy, on that day I wished to know more than that.

When we went out to buy food, we found the houses on our way to the store in the corner loud with the news. At the store, standby revolutionaries were discussing the possibility of the president's flight.

The world had gone on marvelously without us.

FERNANDO AND I rode to the spilling street on his motorbike. We rode via Kamias, then right down through Epifanio de los Santos Avenue, where the saints were marching in. They wore silk stockings and baseball caps, sneakers and sarongs. We drove past a girl in convent school uniform wearing fashionable Ray-Ban shades. She stopped to buy peanuts from a traveling peddler, who, like her, wore a hat with a yellow plastic hand atop it, with the double-digit sign, thumb and finger shaping the letter L: *Laban, Laban, Laban!* Fight, fight, fight. It looked like a souvenir for some basketball varsity team. Everyone sounded like a cheering squad in a college dorm.

The foam icons on people's yellow heads looked sprightly, though ready to topple.

Our revolt was this vast theater of mundane jubilations.

At the corner near Cubao Farmer's Plaza, we came upon a barricade. A lone, empty bus. We got off and began to walk. We met: street urchins with cigarettes to sell, unwashed college students who had slept on the street in sweaters and thick socks, and Jon, a newspaperman I had met once at a party and dumped soon after. He had on a Boston Red Sox baseball cap and was scribbling in a notebook before the empty bus.

"What's up, Jon?" I asked.

"Nothing of concern to you," he said with scorn. "It's just a revolution."

And he continued writing.

I got more information from Manuel Misericordia.

I looked at him, shocked.

"What happened to you?" I asked.

"I'm an editor now," he said, smiling happily, "at the Department of Tourism. My girlfriend came back. She's pregnant. Gotta feed the kid."

He wore this striped, collared shirt and a buzz cut. He used to be a poet in a rage. Now he was a boy with a purpose. He was in a hurry as he explained to me: "I believe that the defense minister really had been planning some plot—if not an outright presidential assassination, perhaps some long-premeditated, urban attack. They thought they could stage a coup and grab power for themselves as people power swelled. Opportunists! Now they've pledged allegiance to Cory and her supporters. They had to. People power is the only way they can survive." He shook his head. "I can't believe I'm on the streets for Marcos's damned defense minister, the designer of martial law."

"For sure, there will be more surprises to come," I said to him. "Scum in your anus and pus in your balls!"

He laughed and waved me on. He strode ahead of us.

We passed a banner that said: "Ipil-Ipil Residence Hall for Democracy and Justice." Another said: "Ateneo Zoology Club for Justice and Reconciliation." Behind this sign, a group of men and women, every single one of them in yellow shirts and brown penny loafers, or their favored Sperry, and looking exactly like their vaunted enemies, the La Sallistas across the street. They all shared umbrellas and more peanuts and waved the two-fingered *L* sign as we passed.

Awkward and inexperienced, I waved back.

But I was clumsy and showed them the wrong fingers.

This cheeriness was new to me.

A tidy man in Adidas running shoes was busy with a slew of customers. He was in his thirties, and he had a bushel of boiled peanuts, smoking sweetly in the morning air and stashed upon a wooden cart. He had on a many-pocketed apron and was casting money into it. As soon as one customer was done, another flag-bearing street rebel ordered another bag.

"I know him." I nudged Fernando. Fernando had found a friend of his, a clarinetist whose shirt proclaimed: "U.P. Musical Ensemble for Cory."

Fernando turned from the clarinetist, who was explaining the contrapuntal rhythms with which one could play "Ang Bayan Ko," to look at the peanut seller.

"He's a former teacher of mine," I whispered to him.

"Oh, yeah," Fernando noted. "I had him for English 3. He was a pathetic stutterer, man. He spewed when he spoke. No one wanted to sit in the front row."

"Good morning, sir," I said to my teacher.

"Ah, M-m-miss P-p-pereg-g-g-rino," said my teacher brightly. "Great day, isn't it? Business has never been better. What do you think of my p-part-time job? It beats teaching those g-g-godawful Romantic poets."

"It's a great idea," I said.

"I think th-this is the b-business for me: as W. H. Auden says—p-poetry makes nothing happen. Whereas—look at this!"

He happily opened his arms wide, jingling the coins in his apron. Saliva dribbled busily down his chin.

Farther on, I saw May and several mystics calmly chewing on indeterminate things—something appropriately yellow.

"Excuse me," I told my teacher.

But another customer had already engaged him, and he went off to fill a bag of steaming nuts.

"Primi!"

May was wearing the same blouse I had seen on her two days before. She had a yellow headband in her hair and looked like Alice in Wonderland, but for Cory, waving a corncob in the air.

"Can you believe it? It's finally happening. Our prayers have been answered. Anna must be so proud and excited. It's exactly as she said it would be: And a star will lead us. Look."

I looked up to where she was pointing. I saw a wide, anonymous sky over the metropolis, blue and unclouded. The gray shapes of crowds and falling confetti had dispersed from the heavens. Now the world looked as fresh as nobody's scrubbed skin.

"It's a beautiful day," I said. "Exactly as it should be. Anna should be happy."

"She certainly is," said May. "She's a celebrity now, an EDSA saint. But don't you see?"

And one of the mystics, the bookseller from Beijing, pointed with his index of corn to some form in the sky.

"It's Halley's Comet," he said. He shielded his eyes from the sky's glare. "It has been over the city the entire night. Hasn't been seen in seventy-six years, since 1910. And it will appear again maybe eighty years from now. Who knows, maybe the country will be different then, ruled by the proletariat. Isn't that something? It's a sign. Halley's Comet. Just as your sister predicted—and a star will lead us. She's something else, is Anna. You'll see it better in the evening."

I didn't see a thing. But at this point, I thought it might be best to trust their vision.

I was overwhelmed by the massed sense of giddy yet frightened expectation, palpable all along the street.

Up and down Epifanio de los Santos Avenue, the epiphany on EDSA, crowds were swelling, strolling, ogling. Office workers in straw hats, layabouts in slippers, nuns, nurses, lawyers carrying backpacks and lovers holding hands. A seminarian held aloft a gigantic white cross. Flocks of women in the blue sash and white shifts of Our Lady of Lourdes followed him—a passing drone of prayer. Ladies held paper bags along with their rosaries. Everyone was prepared for both miracles and lunch. I sidestepped them. When I emerged from a crowd of socialites in high, teased hairdos and lowly, yellow shirts, I found I'd lost Fernando. I saw, among a crowd sitting before the secured gates of Camp Aguinaldo, a beggar with his begging can full of leaflets, a score of what seemed to be schoolchildren unpacking their snacks, and a plastic tent with a red cross on it. By a table outside the tent, a white-clothed intern was listening to the radio, fanning herself.

Where once traffic had clogged this street, the longest thoroughfare in Metro Manila, people now held power. A five-mile traffic of residents going about their daily business, making change and eating peanuts—this was the city's revolution.

To change the fate of the country all they needed was to arrive.

"Where's Somerset?" I asked May, when the holy procession had passed.

"He's gone home," May said. "He has to sort out in his head what he's just seen. He's in shock, poor guy."

I moved closer to the gates of the military camp. On one side was Camp Aguinaldo, where the general and the defense minister had holed up; on the right was Camp Crame, where the dictator's men had ranged. There were streamers on the gates, demanding a full gamut of restoration, cleansing, fall, justice, and condemnation. *Imperialismo, ibagsak*. Justice for Ninoy, Justice for All. Student Catholic Action. Farmers' groups. Reform the Armed Forces Movement. Florists of Manila, Blooming for Cory! Beauticians and botanists demanded National Reconciliation. The city wore its passion on its gates. And atop the pillars, roaming about the camp's ramparts, were the soldiers who had defected.

"The defective soldiers," a man beside me quipped.

It was Domingo Cantero, poet and metallic bookmark collector.

He looked as troubled as ever.

He had his large hands on his face, covering his bony cheeks. He did not look at me, and then he didn't speak.

"Hello," I said.

Then he said: "It's a kind of salvation, I suppose."

"For the country?" I asked.

"Maybe not," he said. "But maybe for some of us—an act of contrition. For our own private lapses."

I decided to move on.

Then a unanimous sound came through the crowd. A murmur.

I turned back. We both had to stand on tiptoe to look.

We watched the same scene: a soldier with a flower in the bore of his M-16. A student had presented him with a yellow rose. I noticed that the soldier had the Philippine flag patched on his sleeve. It was sewn upside down, the red field up.

The upside down flag: it sent shivers through me, despite myself.

It was the sign of war.

A lady offered this soldier a sandwich. He shook his head, self-consciously implacable upon his sentry wall.

I said to Domingo: "I'm not exactly sure if one should laugh or cry at this part of the story."

"Should we simply take it in its spirit, burying all our hatchets?" he said, with the strangest look of hope, holding out his hand.

I had to smile. I shook his hand. I moved on. I waved goodbye.

OF COURSE, I saw Anna on these streets.

She was with her increasing phalanx of supporters. They wore flowing white robes like her and were ready to accomplish her every bidding. Journalists sought her opinion on the next possible events.

I found ubiquitous Jon, the newsman with the notebook, interviewing her.

"So, when do you think the dictator will flee?"

"Tomorrow morning at half past seven," said Anna. "He believes in sevens, you know, in the comfort of numerology. But he'll find that his own numbers will destroy him."

"What do you mean?"

"He had planned his election coup on February 7th: but that only created this tidal wave you see here. He had written out his drama to arrest coup plotters on February 21."

"What does that have to do with seven?"

"Ah: I see you are a journalist. Twenty-one is a multiple of seven, as anyone might note. Quite symmetrical with the martial law date: September 21, 1972."

"Also a multiple of seven. But 1972?"

"Don't worry about that: that was a historical necessity: you can't have numbers mean something all of the time. September, by the way, is rooted in the Latin word for seven, though it is the ninth month of the year. Coincidentally, that was the date of my parents' death."

"Ah," said Jon, scribbling away. "Is that correct?" he asked. "Were they rebels, your parents?"

"They were martyrs of Tacloban."

"Where the First Lady is from," Jon said, nodding, "the woman behind the assassination of Cory's husband."

Jon was writing fast.

"They gave up their lives in 1972. They fell from the side of a ship. Their bodies have never been found. At the onset of martial law, in 1972, they protested this coil of life, our country's sadness."

My heart was in my throat.

People in the white robes were nodding, solemn, as if hearing about the Resurrection.

"Or—" and I could see Anna's broad smile, glancing over a believing crowd—"it could also have been a coincidence." At this point, I thought Anna had seen me. I started backing away, but Anna did not waver from her gaze on the journalist.

"Anyway," she said, "1986 is exactly fourteen years after his martial law triumph. Yet another multiple of seven. Fourteen, got it? February 21, 1986, was most auspicious, then, for the dictator. But contrary to his well-reasoned fate, his victims eluded him. The people rejected his numerology. He believes he can last this out until an appropriate time, say the 27th, or the seventh day after this revolt. Or, you know, the twelfth of never. Because we will outwit him. On the 24th, he will leave—it's not a number divisible by seven, as you know. It's an eternal contradiction of his symbols. He will never come back."

When Jon left, a television host joined her.

A crewman beamed a white spotlight upon Anna, rendering quite literal the colors of her aura.

I moved on.

I almost bumped into Sabado. I recognized him by the thickness of his glasses and his buttoned-up shirt.

He was with Anna's coven of believers. He wore white loose

pants and his shirt was uncharacteristically tucked out. A girl in white sat beside him as he arranged candles around a makeshift tent made of woven talahib and newsprint, before the Camp Crame walls. Of course, Anna's group had arrived even before the Archbishop of Manila had summoned everyone onto the street and thus maintained this choice revolutionary spot: with a close view of center stage, and yet their own space for contemplation and rest.

I almost fell over Sabado and the girl. I accidentally extinguished their candles.

"Well, hi," Sabado said, standing up and shaking dirt from his hands. "Primi. Good to see you here. This is Janine."

The girl nodded gravely. She tried to relight the candles.

"I've joined your sister's sect."

"I see."

"I have also changed my ways," Sabado said.

"How?"

"I am getting married," he confided, taking me aside. He gestured toward Janine. "We will not have sex until after our ceremony. We will do it all correctly, in cleanness and light."

"I'm happy for you. Good luck."

The girl had managed to strike a match smartly, and with one flicker, a candle came to life, then sputtered.

Even for Sabado, one felt an overflowing kindness, part of the trance on the street.

I moved on. So did the day's activity. I kept walking down the long, straight street. It was a simple, vertical plot. Epifanio de los Santos Avenue stretched quite plainly ahead, without tangent or diversion.

IT WAS AT about this time, I believe, that the country became afflicted with what one might call *semiosis*, a sepsis of the semiotic tract, an infection of the sign-making glands. We assign to this event meanings that all lead to questions of life and death, philosophical heartburn and patriotic dread. We revise and revisit our feelings toward it the way Romans of old found omens in the intestines of birds. That, too, was a form of semiosis. The street itself, EDSA, takes on, at odd moments in the present day when I travel through it, a weirdly disorienting sense of a symbol gone awry. Why should it? It's still just a street, going to seed in an unremarkable third world way.

Other people (e.g., psychoanalysts, romance novelists, air traffic controllers) have pointed out before in different contexts that the ability to see meanings is not necessarily a sign of wisdom, or health. It may indicate intellectual training or acumen, yes, but it may also be a symptom of delusion, fierce heartache, severe ennui, and other renditions of mental weakness. We must take into account that our own revisions of the rebellion we call, eponymously and thoughtlessly, *EDSA* may be all of the above, and more.

If it is at all possible, in a non-Heraclitean world, to go back, to step into the same river twice, maybe when we do we must ban all meanings, tropes, and symbols—the maladies afflicting EDSA. Maybe if we can stem memory within some filtering contraption, a device of a sort for disinfection, by which we can flush out metonyms, similes, ugly gigantic memorial statues, newspaper editorials, biblical references, mythical allusions, and this entire paragraph, maybe then we might distill something more pure and light, closer to the original weight of a single minute on that street.

The problem with epiphanies is that by definition they cannot be shared. There was no national epiphany in February of 1986; there may have been a million revelations lodged quietly and inarticulately in each heart.

Which may be a flaw in the message, if you wish to see it that way.

THERE SEEMED NO visible increase of excitement, except for one moment when a Camp Crame gate opened. A group of soldiers in fatigue, Philippine flag patch red side up, came out of the Camp in single file, solemnly hefting a bazooka. The machine was about the size of a baby: a grim phallic organ that cut cleanly through the ranks. A collective gasp—or was it a sigh—came through the crowd. It was the high point of our day.

No one knew its destination, though everyone asked.

I continued on my way, following the yellow-lined road.

As I walked on, I saw more people whom I knew—students,

poets' wives, beatnik leftovers with acned skin and lovely hair, poetesses, blissful gay people holding hands instead of banners, fortunetelling fictionists, and many sweet, messy men.

Later, I met Uncle Diego in a dim curve close to Makati.

I didn't recognize him at first. It was close to twilight, and the moon was rising as the sun lingered. The light would soon throw off an odd glow—an unwelcome patina of beauty. Soon, the street was to be wrapped in a tender gleam that would seem too aesthetically configured, a cinematographer's *retoke*, giving the scene the slightly repulsive charm of perfectly lit beauty.

Uncle Diego was holding a moviecam, intent on taking footage of a group of girls selling corn on the cob. They wore the yellow shirts of the event, and, as Uncle Diego took aim, they waved the correct construct of fingers.

I recognized it was Uncle Diego by the concave fixedness of his spine when he straightened. Otherwise, he looked different: bearded and bellied.

"Uncle Diego!" I said.

His eye didn't move from the camera.

I waited for him to finish.

"Punyeta," he said when he looked up. "Just as the pictures are getting good, the light changes. Well, Primi, of course, you're here. Every other damned maiden of my life has passed by, why not you, too?"

And he reached out to kiss me.

"Well, what do you think," he said, holding out his arms so I could see his wealth better.

"You look healthy. Have you quit managing starlets?"

"I quit babysitting a long time ago. Now I make movies of my own."

"You look good," I said. "How's the moviemaking?"

"Need you ask? This is a New Critic's gold mine and a post-structuralist's nightmare—every scene is ready for commentary and reduction." Uncle Diego had clearly taken courses. He took my arm and we sat on the pavement. He replaced his camera carefully into its case. "Can you believe what happened to Anna? Your sister as EDSA celebrity? I keep seeing her as a child—on that nearly fatal hunger strike."

The glow of twilight softened the twitch on the street, it seemed. People were slowing down.

They were setting out their blankets and statues of the Virgin and Saint Joseph. They set up icons of bloodied Christs to guard against the promised guns.

Evening brought out a relish for death.

We had been told to stay overnight, expecting danger.

"Anna gave me some cartoons a while ago," I said. "She said you had given them to her. She thinks that Prospero was a rebel. She thinks he's one in a line of pre-EDSA saints."

"Anibal the Ipis." Uncle Diego nodded. "Nice work. Your father believed those were his best pieces—and he still didn't think they were any good. I thought at first that was why he killed himself—because of his morbid, strict notions of craft. He was like that, you know. He thought those Voltes V cartoons were a joke, for instance: unworthy of his talents."

"Really? You thought he died because of his art? Anna says my father killed himself to protest martial law."

Uncle Diego shrugged. "Anything's possible. But no, Primi, my answer to the question you're not asking is: I don't know why your parents decided to jump ship—though their reasons haunt me. It's strange how times like this make one think even more strongly of our own stuff—our own lives. Every day I miss your father. I can't fathom at all why anyone would do what he did. His children needed him. I don't understand your mother. Why she left you and Anna. It makes me sad. But Primi—we will read ourselves in everyone's motions, we will try to interpret others' worlds through our eyes. It is all we have. And even the most impartial eye will have only partial glimpses, or something limited but compassionate, or something complete yet ironic: which in itself is a limitation. Or something full of gibberish and stubbly thoughts—like myself right now.

"I discussed this with Anna before—she has that frame of mind certain people have. They want a definitive answer, they want links within a story, a clear thread of plot. But she's smart, Primi—she sticks to her version. It's a form of sanity. We can let her be. You have your own version. Let that be."

"But, Uncle Diego," I said, holding on to his arm. "I have no version. I keep thinking of my mother and father in bits and pieces of flashbacks and faulty memory."

"Is that so bad?"

I thought about it. Would it be so horrible if, one day, this week in February turned out to be a mistaken prelude to the nation's fall? Would it eliminate the days' strange glory if it turned out to be a mere piece in the puzzle, a blip in a more difficult history?

Would it be so bad if one did not know the cause of one's parents' death, except for one's own limited ways of remembrance, of tracing out ways to recall how much one was loved?

"Call me old and crazy, Primi. Maybe that's all we need to know about people. The bits and pieces we wish to keep. The love we bear them anyhow, no matter that we cannot bear the way they died, because we remember how they lived. Hearsay and desire are all I have. Apart from these, we have no other weapons, except to keep trying to remember as much as we can. With love. I am so sorry, Primi, that that is all I have."

He stood up and gestured to me. "Now, would you like a bite to eat? I'm sick of peanuts and corn. I wish this event had been better planned. The entire goddamned EDSA menu sticks to my teeth."

WE FOUND A place along EDSA, darkly lit but open to customers.

Uncle Diego was telling me: "I don't know about you, Primi, but I've heard sorrowful things about you on the grapevine."

"Such as?"

"I hear you went out with a certain former official of public information. The dictator's own private stooge."

"That was only for a couple of nights, Uncle Diego. I didn't really like him."

"I should hope not. He's around, you know."

In fact, on the restaurant TV, there he was: Huevos Santo. Mr. Holy Eggs himself.

He had become a foreign news agency's commentator on the dictator's next moves. Rumors said the former official was planning to buy a news station of his own. His ophidian skin crawled upon the screen like a plastered gob, the smeared imprint of a scaly claw.

"Sickening," I said as I speared my sisig. The plate of skewered pig's-ears, slashed and onioned, was my favorite. It looked like unprocessed digestion but had the texture and taste of flesh in rich season. I ate hungrily.

CNN had cornered the market on the street revolt. I looked at the onscreen crowds. The country had emerged as kitsch of the day, a panorama of many divisible scenes shot up as one gigantic yellow mushroom you could chew, and psychedelia followed.

"Isn't it suspect?" said a man behind me.

Of course, it was Somerset.

He had always favored this eatery on EDSA. It was the same sausage bar that had once hosted a poetry reading.

Today, Polish kielbasa was on glittering display: it was the form and sheen, in fact, of a tinny bazooka. Meals were robust and abundant. People were relaxing from their hard day at the revolution.

"Suspect in what way?" asked Uncle Diego.

"All our symbols are an easy lay. Every scene is sellable. Every person you meet on the street is a character caught up in a novel whose end they have yet to figure out. But that's so much the better. So say all the smug commentators. Suspense! That creates ratings! We're the market place for sound bites. You could talk about the country's signs endlessly. Right now as we speak semioticians are going mad. You don't need fairy tales—just come right up to EDSA.

"I suppose one can't help it if real life ends up being a clunky book," he continued, ranting, "with a writer mad for symbols and reversals, dictator's goon turned savior, housewife turned angel, The Saints Come Marching In on stilettos and piled Clairol Hi and Dry hairdos. It's ridiculous. None of this—" And he swept his hand across the television screen, "would hold up in a good book.

"I'm not writing a single word more," said Somerset, taking a swig of Guinness, the new imported luxury he allowed himself, now that he had given up on his country. "I'm selling used clothing and starting a business in computer graphics. You won't hear another word from me. I still think my own version was better—the spilling of guts and blood, cousin against cousin, brother against brother, and in the end, no one wins, but boy, what a battle! That should be the fate of the nation.

That's tragic! That's artistic karma! Not this low-frequency electromagnetic feast of saints. Slipshod, heavy-handed, cheesy EDSA script."

"That's all right, Somerset," I said, sipping from his beer. "Maybe your story's time will come. Take it as another Palanca loss: you've been beaten by other plotters, the people of your country. Now buy us another round of beer."

LATER I FOUND Fernando at his motorbike, waiting for my arrival.

I had called him the penultimate boy, because Fernando didn't last. Nothing did.

On the twenty-fourth, as Anna had prophesied, the news traveled through the streets that the dictator had left. I recall dancing with a stranger in a red shirt, doing a kind of cha-cha in a wild, out-of-tune surprise. We swirled and pivoted and when we found ourselves separated, we clapped. The stranger then bowed to me as the street continued to buzz: the dictator had left, airlifted out of the palace.

Soon, of course, we discovered our error. On television, the man was still in our midst. We had danced to a false alarm. The rumors of his departure were sadly exaggerated.

Where had the news come from, the columnists asked? Perhaps from a mystic of goddess proportions, who disappeared that morning of the twenty-fourth—practically leaving with the comet.

It was the next day that he left, the twenty-fifth, airlifted out of our lives by Ronald Reagan.

I KEEP WONDERING where Anna is now—where she has taken her potent gifts. I miss her. She was the only family I had.

Sometimes I freeze-frame that morning, when mistakenly we believed that all trials were over—I see this country in this motion-picture pause, trapped in the festivity of a long false alarm.

AND EVEN AS I put down this pen, I know I'm dis-anchoring once again—I'm sailing. I'm looking for the final word, the book at the end of my journey.

"It's as if you're searching for some body you've lost," my doctor said, "a body in the ocean. And words are all you have to show for it."

I sat in this room in Makati. The doctor seemed quite impressed by the neatness of her thoughts.

"Write it out," she said brightly. "Write it. That's always good therapy for matters of loss."

LIKE ANY CITIZEN in a passionate country, I keep looking for some chimera. In my case, that fabulous monster of incongruous parts—text and body, manual and man. Meanwhile, all I have is this wandering, reading's endlessly replenishable boon.

Dressed still in his black bicycle jacket, washed and shaven, Fernando was turning the pages of an oversized book.

"Where did you go?" I asked.

He shrugged. "Borrowed a book."

"In the middle of the country's upheaval?"

"Well, the British Council was open. Look what I found."

It was a book in facsimile, the novel in the writer's own taut, slanted hand.

"See how precise and fine his script was," Fernando said, his bright face glowing. "Can you think of what love went into this?"